SYNOPSIS

Ben and Rob are in love. They met in Barcelona a year ago and fell for each other on a Mediterranean cruise. Since then, they've spent as much time as possible together, and that's no easy task since they live on opposites sides of the country.

After celebrating Thanksgiving together and deciding to spend Christmas at Ben's family home in England, Ben and Rob start rethinking their long-distance love story. But what's a family holiday without drama?

When Ben's brother brings an important issue to light, the result may be the next step Ben and Rob are waiting for. And what better way to celebrate the Christmas season than with family, good friends, special gifts, and a decision that could change Ben and Rob's lives.

Love FOR THE HOLIDAYS

NEW ADVENTURES IN LOVE · BOOK 2

RJ Peterson

Love for the Holidays

New Adventures in Love, Book 2

No Generative AI Training Use.

For avoidance of doubt, Author reserves the rights, and does not grant permission to any individual/company/publisher/platform any rights to reproduce and/or otherwise use the Work in any manner for purposes of training artificial intelligence technologies to generate text, including without limitation, technologies that are capable of generating works in the same style or genre as the Work, unless said individual/company/publisher/platform obtains Author's specific and express permission to do so. Nor does any individual/company/publisher/platform have the right to sublicense others to reproduce and/or otherwise use the Work in any manner for purposes of training artificial intelligence technologies to generate text without Author's specific and express permission.

In addition, no artificial intelligence (A.I.), predictive language software, or generative design software was used in any part of the creation of this book or its cover, nor will it ever be for any of my works.

To Sharon.

We began as co-workers and soon became friends.
Now I'm proud to call you family.

"Family isn't always blood. It's the people in your
life who want you in theirs.
The ones who accept you for who you are.
The ones who would do anything
to see you smile & who love you
no matter what."

CONTENTS

A WORD ABOUT COVID

When I wrote my first book, Love On The Horizon, I wasn't expecting it to become a series, so I purposely set it in the fall of 2019, thus avoiding any reference to COVID-19. But then, something interesting happened...

As I continued to write that first book, I started to get ideas for additional stories in the same universe. Once I published Love On The Horizon, I started this book and made a decision. The New Adventures in Love series will all take place in a parallel universe that is exactly like the world we live in—except there's no COVID pandemic.

We've all suffered enough in so many ways over the past two years or so, and I thought it might be nice for this series to be an escape from all of that.

ACKNOWLEDGMENTS

While my name appears on the cover, it's really a team effort. There are so many people who helped make this book possible...

David, my husband, friend, and travel partner. Thanks for your support and for continuing to make me laugh for 41+ years. Here's to new adventures and many more laughs!

Karen D. Bonnick, my friend, mentor, and colleague – thanks for everything.

Dianne Thies, thank you once again for putting up with this newbie author. You take my words and make them so much better. You also fix all those pesky punctuation errors and I'm truly grateful!

Dr. Charlotte V. Carrington-Farmer, friend and UK-native. As my personal British encyclopedia, thank you for your edits, corrections, and suggestions. Despite all of your help, any errors in this book are mine and mine alone.

Sammi Cee, your guidance helped make this book immeasurably better. Thank you from the bottom of my heart.

K-lee Klein, I owe you so many hugs for all of your support. Your suggestions were exactly what I needed. Thank you, my friend.

Tricia Morris, friend, boss, teacher, and now reader. Is there anything you can't do? Huge thanks for your continued support.

Melissa Brus, your friendship and support are beyond measure. I owe you hugs. And tequila!

T.S. McKinney, you're crazy and I love you. Thank you for believing in me. And yes, I owe you drinks. Many, many drinks!

Brandon Witt-Schoen, thank you once again for letting me borrow The Cozy Corgi Mysteries and Mildred Abbott so that folks had something to read and talk about while in England together. Your friendship and support mean so very much to me.

Last, but not least, to all the authors who have inspired and entertained me over the years: Gregory Ashe, Michael Bailey, Tal Bauer, Hank Edwards, Rhys Ford, Jordan L. Hawk, Davidson King, Alexa Land, Ann Lister, Angel Martinez, Annabella Michaels, C.S. Poe, and so many more – huge thanks for the laughter, tears, & angst. But most importantly, immense gratitude for your friendship and support.

PROLOGUE

"I can't believe it's already been a year since we were on the *Ocean Wanderer*. Time flies when you're in love, I guess." Ben sighed, feeling more relaxed than he'd been in a long time.

Peering lovingly at Rob, he added, "I'm so glad you talked me into taking this cruise. I needed this vacation more than I realized. I'm just sad that we'll be back in New York in a couple of days." The gentle breeze felt like a lover's caress as they sat out on the balcony, enjoying the warmth of the sun and their view of an endless sapphire sea.

"I know what you mean, sweetie. This was a wonderful way to celebrate our first anniversary, even if we are a few weeks late," Rob said.

Two weeks earlier, Ben had finished a three-month run of the play *Betrayal* by Harold Pinter at New York's Broadhurst Theatre. It had been a grueling schedule with eight performances a week, and they hadn't been able to spend a lot of time together, but once it was over, Rob surprised him with this week-long cruise to Bermuda. It was the perfect way to wind down.

"When the play ended, you were exhausted. It made sense to just relax for a while, and what better way than on a cruise?" Rob continued.

"You're right, of course. But you didn't have to splurge on a Nautilus Suite," Ben replied excitedly. "I didn't even know they offered cabins like this with a bedroom loft. It's incredible."

"I just figured that if you wanted to really escape for a week, you should be able to do it in comfort," Rob said. "And since we only left the ship once, we did get to enjoy the suite a bit more than usual."

"Especially the bedroom." Ben winked. "Although I'm really glad we got off the ship at King's Wharf and went to The Frog and Onion Tuesday afternoon. Those Dark 'n' Stormies were delicious."

"That they were."

The ship wasn't quite as large as the one they sailed on the year before when they met in Barcelona, but it was just as tasteful and elegant. And their suite was no exception. Decorated in seafoam green, navy, and tan, it featured a living room with a small dining area, large balcony, and guest bathroom on the first floor, with a staircase leading up to the loft bedroom and large master bath. The balcony wall offered floor-to-ceiling windows, so you could even gaze upon the ocean from the loft while lying in bed.

"We've got a reservation at the Poseidon Steakhouse for dinner tonight. Maybe we could head out early and stop for a drink in the Suite Lounge before we eat. Is that okay with you?" Rob asked.

"That's fine. What time is the reservation?"

"Eight forty-five, why?"

"Well then, we have more than enough time before dinner. Wanna get dirty with me before we clean up?" Ben grinned.

"That sounds perfect," Rob agreed, dragging Ben off the balcony and up the stairs.

Friday, October 23 – aboard Ocean Voyager

AFTER A LEISURELY SHOWER TOGETHER, Ben and Rob made their way to the Bluefin Bistro on Deck 14 for breakfast. Located on the starboard side of the ship, it offered some great ocean views along with superb food. Ben realized they'd dined there quite a bit during this cruise, as the hostess greeted them by name then seated them at a window table so they could enjoy the brilliant azure sea and cloudless sky while they tucked into their meal.

After placing an order with their server, they sat back and enjoyed their coffee.

"So what's on today's agenda?" Ben asked, knowing full

well that Rob had already consulted the daily schedule. That was just the way he was, and Ben loved that he found so much pleasure in planning and organizing their trips.

"I was going to see if I could get appointments at the Thermal Spa this morning. A soak in the therapy pool and a sauna would be so relaxing. You interested?"

"Definitely," Ben enthused. "I really enjoyed the time we spent there earlier this week."

"There's a wine tasting in Neptune's Wine Bar after lunch. I was thinking we could attend. Then we can relax on our balcony. After all, that's what this vacation is all about, right?"

"You're absolutely correct," Ben replied. "And we should be sure to make a reservation here tonight. As much as I enjoy the specialty restaurants on board, I really love this place."

"Certainly," Rob agreed. "We can talk to the hostess on our way out."

AT FIVE PAST SEVEN, Ben and Rob strolled hand in hand into the Suite Lounge and found it surprisingly crowded. It seemed folks were taking advantage of everything the ship had to offer on the last night of the cruise. As they walked toward the bar, a couple was just leaving, so Ben and Rob quickly commandeered the now-empty seats.

"Good evening, Mr. Ben, Mr. Rob." Renata smiled as she placed a cruise-line-logoed napkin in front of each of them. "The usual?"

"Yes, please." Ben laughed. They'd obviously spent a lot of time there in the past seven days.

The bartender quickly and expertly mixed a Manhattan for Ben and a vodka martini for Rob.

"*Salud.* Enjoy your beverages, gentlemen." Renata placed the drinks and a small bowl of snacks before them.

"This never gets old." Rob sighed, clinked his glass with Ben's, then sipped his ice-cold martini.

"Too true, my dear," Ben agreed. "Maybe we should plan our next one. Something in the spring, perhaps?"

"Oh my God, I've turned you into a cruise whore, haven't I?" Rob joked.

"Ha! You've just shown me what I've been missing out on, and I'm trying to make up for lost time." Ben chuckled, thinking of how much things had changed in the last year. Rob had made him realize that it was time to enjoy life more. Hopefully that meant a life that included Rob.

"Fine. I'll ask Sam to look for something in the spring. Maybe a crossing if you think you'll have the time—we'd need about three weeks."

"That sounds okay. You know I'm not interested in doing anything else workwise for a while. I need to talk to Amanda when we get back, but I don't think it'll be a problem."

"Excellent. I've been meaning to talk to you about something." Rob paused, collecting his thoughts. "I'm seriously considering selling the condo in Florida. Alan and I bought it to have a place to go in the winter, but I couldn't go back after he died. I mean, you and I have only stayed there once, and it just doesn't feel like a place I want to keep anymore."

"If you're not happy with it, then sure, selling it is probably the right thing to do," Ben agreed. "If we decide that Florida is somewhere we want to spend more time, we can look for something else to buy together. But there's no rush. Hotels and rentals work for any vacation we'd want to take."

"Okay ... good. I'll call the sales office at the condo next week."

Their glasses finally empty, they left the lounge and walked hand in hand to their final dinner of the cruise.

CHAPTER 1

Wednesday, November 25 – the day before Thanksgiving

"Sweetheart, are you ready?" Ben called up to the second floor as he pulled on his coat. "I don't want to be late."

"Relax, we've got plenty of time," Rob said, descending the stairs. He paused, kissing Ben on the lips. "Kyle's plane lands in an hour, and it won't take that long to get to the airport."

"I know, I'm just excited to see him. And before you say anything, FaceTime on Monday doesn't count."

Rob chuckled, holding up the key fob. "Fine. Do you want to drive?"

"No, I like being chauffeured." Ben handed Rob his jacket, and they stepped through the kitchen and into the garage. Ben set the alarm while Rob hit the button to open the garage door, then they were off to T.F. Green International Airport in Rhode Island, forty minutes away.

They waited in the cell phone lot until Ben got a text from Kyle saying he was walking out the doors to the pick-up area. When they saw Kyle, Ben immediately hopped out of the car and waved enthusiastically. Kyle definitely looked like Ben, although at five feet seven inches, he was a bit shorter and leaner. His hair was dirty blond and cut short, but he shared Ben's piercing green eyes.

"Hey son, good to see you." He wrapped Kyle in a bear hug and kissed him on the cheek. Grabbing Kyle's luggage, he tossed it in the back of Rob's SUV as Kyle got in the back seat.

"Hi Rob, how are you doin'?" Kyle asked as he reached over and squeezed Rob's shoulder.

"Good, Kyle. How are you? Your dad's been stressing all day about picking you up."

"You've met him, right?" Kyle laughed.

"Hey, I'm right here," Ben chimed in as he sat in the front seat. "Don't be a smart ass. Both of you."

"We tease you because we love you, Dad."

Ben turned in his seat, smiling. "How was your flight?"

"Fine. There's barely enough time to get in the air, and they're already planning the descent. I love these short flights."

They chatted aimlessly to pass the time, and before too long, Rob was pulling into the driveway.

The three of them entered the kitchen where Kyle knelt beside his bag and unzipped it. Pulling out a bottle of wine, he handed it to Rob and said, "I'm a bit late, but happy anniversary! It's been a year for you and my dad, right?"

Rob inspected the bottle, saying, "Thank you, Kyle. Yeah, it was a year last month." He looked at the label and saw that it was a Manto Negro. "Wait a minute," he said, glancing at Ben. "Is this the wine we had in Barcelona?"

Ben blushed. "If Kyle was able to find it, then yes. It's the one we had at the tapas restaurant the day we met. Remember, you took a photo of it that night? I may have sent the photo to Kyle in hopes that he could find a bottle."

Rob marveled at how much Ben paid attention to little things–like remembering the wine they drank a year ago–and turned it into something special that they could both share.

"I had to order it since the wine shop I went to didn't carry it, but yes, that's the same wine," Kyle admitted.

Rob pulled Kyle into a hug. "Thank you so much. This means a lot to me, well, to us." Rob wiped at his eyes, feeling quite emotional. He hugged Ben and kissed him tenderly. "Thank you too, sweetie."

"I can't remember the last time I've seen my dad this happy, so thank you for everything you've done, Rob. Not that I want to hear any of those details, 'cause I really can't afford the therapy bills," Kyle joked.

"Don't worry, Kyle. I don't kiss and tell," Rob said, smiling.

***

Thursday, November 26 – Thanksgiving Day

After sipping his coffee, Rob beat eggs together with milk, sugar, vanilla, and cinnamon for his famous French toast casserole. The bacon and sausage were already cooked and now sat in the warming oven. He finished preparing the casserole and slid it into the oven. Setting a timer, he got the orange juice and sparkling wine out of the refrigerator—Samantha would be there shortly, and Rob had agreed to supply mimosas while they prepared their Thanksgiving feast together. Hearing footsteps on the stairs, he turned to see Ben and Kyle enter the kitchen.

"Good morning, sweetheart." Ben kissed him, then stole a sip from Rob's coffee cup.

"Hey, get your own coffee," Rob complained. "And while you're at it, top mine off and also get a cup for Kyle, please."

Turning to his son, Ben asked, "Did you sleep okay?"

"I did, thanks." Kyle took a swig from the mug that Ben handed him. "What can I do to help?"

"Nothing yet," Rob answered. "Breakfast will be ready in a little while. Sam should be here soon, and after we eat, we can start in on the food prep for dinner. For now, just relax and enjoy your coffee."

"I'm really looking forward to meeting her," Kyle said. "I know we've talked on FaceTime on a few occasions, but it's not quite the same."

Just then, the doorbell rang. Ben opened the breezeway door, and Sam stood there, her arms laden with flowers and wine. "Happy Thanksgiving, guys," she said brightly, handing the wine to Ben. "There's more stuff in my car. Can you get the box on the back seat, please, Ben?"

"Sure. But before I do, it's time for an official introduction. Sam, this is my son Kyle. Kyle, this is Samantha."

Kyle stood and reached out his hand in greeting, but Sam pulled him into a hug and bussed his cheek. "None of that handshaking shit, Kyle. We're family, and I love hugs." She put the flowers on the kitchen island, then turned to Rob and hugged and kissed him. "I don't know what you're cooking, but it smells delicious."

"It's French toast casserole. There are sausages and bacon in the warming oven too. The makings for mimosas are on the counter."

"Perfect." Sam moved around the kitchen, obviously familiar with where everything was. She pulled plates out of a cupboard and flatware from a drawer, then quickly set the round table in the breakfast nook. Grabbing some champagne flutes, she opened the sparkling wine and made four mimosas.

"My dad was right," Kyle said, chuckling. "You are amazing."

"Why, thank you, kind sir," Sam replied. Turning to Ben, she smiled. "I like him already. Ya did good, Papa."

The timer dinged. "Breakfast is ready," Rob announced. Together they put all the food on the table, including a bowl of fruit salad from the fridge.

Lifting his mimosa into the air, Rob toasted. "Here's to family." They clinked glasses and tucked in.

AFTER BREAKFAST AND CLEANUP, Rob assigned tasks to everyone, and they began prepping their Thanksgiving feast.

Ben put the turkey in the oven while Sam and Kyle peeled and chopped various vegetables. Rob prepared the dressing from memory—he'd made this particular recipe so many times, he knew it by heart. He removed breakfast sausage from its casing and sautéed it along with diced onions, carrots, celery, and a Granny Smith apple. He added chopped pecans and dried cranberries, then mixed it all with bread stuffing and chicken stock. Once combined, he spooned it into a buttered casserole dish and popped it into the fridge. He'd place it in the oven for the last hour that the turkey cooked.

After a few hours working together, they finally sat down to a magnificent dinner. They lingered over a dessert of pumpkin and pecan pies, chatting about past holidays and enjoying each other's company.

Rob gazed at Sam, thinking about how their friendship had deepened over the years. Sam had started as Rob & Alan's travel agent, but quickly became a good friend and as time went on, they became family. He was so very thankful that she was part of his and Ben's life.

"Last year when we were on the cruise," Ben began, looking at Rob, "you said you would tell me a story about a time that you and Sam tried to drink at all the bars on the ship in one day. I think it's time you shared, sweetheart."

"Oh, no," Sam groaned. "We're never gonna live that down."

"Yes!" Kyle exclaimed, rubbing his hands together in excitement. "I definitely want to hear about this."

"Fine," said Rob. "Here's what happened. We were on a cruise together in the Caribbean about four or five years ago. It was me, Alan, Sam, and our friend Audrey. Early on in our trip, Sam mentioned that the cruise line limited you to fifteen drinks per day if you had an all-inclusive beverage package. She thought it would be fun to try and have the maximum number of drinks. I foolishly agreed to go along with it, although Audrey and Alan both showed excellent judgement and refrained."

"Clearly not the best idea I've ever had," Sam admitted, shaking her head and smiling.

"We agreed to do it the following day when we'd be at sea. Starting with Bloody Marys at breakfast, it actually began okay. Yes, we bar-hopped, but it was more about how many drinks we were consuming than being on a mission to hit every bar; early on, we did a good job of pacing ourselves."

"But then we went to the aft bar on the pool deck," Sam added. "That's when all hell broke loose."

"Why?" Ben asked. "What happened?"

"I went and opened my big mouth and told the bartender what we were doing," Sam said, shaking her head. "That was our undoing."

"It sure was," Rob continued. "He decided to make us a different shot for each round, and some of them were just awful. It went downhill fast."

"So fucking fast," Sam said with a groan. "It wasn't pretty. Audrey had to help me back to our cabin, and true friend that she is, she may have had to hold my hair up for me while I got sick. Several times."

"I think it was six-thirty when I crashed, and I slept through the night. But at least *I* didn't get sick," Rob said, proudly. "I didn't even have a hangover the next day."

"Don't remind me." Sam stuck her tongue out at Rob, but then she smiled and said proudly, "But we made it to fifteen drinks."

"That we did. But never again."

Ben and Kyle laughed, then Ben said, "I can't imagine

doing something like that. Well, maybe when I was young and foolish, but not just a few years ago."

"Let's just all agree that it wasn't the best decision we ever made," Sam declared. "And let's never speak of this again."

"Okay," Ben said. "Now to change the subject. Kyle, do you have any plans for Christmas yet?"

"No. Why?"

"Rob and I were talking earlier this week, and we thought it might be a good idea to have a family holiday in England this year. Would you be up for that? That goes for you as well, Sam. Wanna come to England with us for Christmas?"

Kyle looked thoughtful. "Yeah, I'd love to do that. It's been a few years since I got to spend any time there. I do have some vacation time left; let me check with my manager on Monday to see if I can take a week or so off."

"I'd love to go!" Sam exclaimed. "I haven't really taken any time off since the cruise last year. I deserve to treat myself."

"Are you thinking of asking Uncle Mike and Aunt Ellen?" Kyle asked.

"Yeah," Ben answered. "In fact, let me call them now and wish them a happy Thanksgiving. At the same time, I can ask Mike about Christmas." He excused himself and walked toward the family room. The rest of them cleaned up the kitchen and dining room.

A little while later, Ben returned and pitched in to help. "Well, that was an interesting conversation."

"Why? What did he say?" Kyle asked.

"He didn't seem overly excited about getting together for Christmas. Wait, that's not quite right. Mike was fine with doing a family holiday but wasn't crazy about the idea of going to England. Frankly, I'm not sure why—he just kind of avoided answering when I asked him. He finally agreed yet didn't seem happy about it. And he said he didn't think Mike Jr. would be able to go, which I can understand, since he and Becky just had a baby, and Mike hasn't been at his job all that long."

"Makes sense about Mike Jr., but yeah, I'm curious about why Uncle Mike doesn't want to go to England. I thought he liked the family home," Kyle said.

"I did too. I'll try and talk to him again next week. Maybe I can get some more information out of him."

Sam left a little while later, promising she'd see them again before Kyle left on Sunday to head back to DC.

"I just can't understand why Mike seemed so resistant to spending Christmas at the family home. He's never reacted like that before." Ben ambled into the bathroom and picked up his toothbrush. "It doesn't make any sense."

"I'm sure you'll get to the bottom of it, sweetheart. Now hurry up and brush your teeth and come to bed." Rob swatted Ben on the ass. "I wanna cuddle."

"I like it when you get bossy," Ben said with a lusty grin before settling into bed beside Rob.

"C'mere." Rob sighed and melted into Ben's body. He inhaled deeply, the scent of orange spice and sandalwood that Ben wore filling his senses. It felt like coming home every time he smelled Ben's cologne.

"I love you so much." They kissed, and even though Rob knew that Ben was still troubled by Mike's attitude about Christmas, for now all was right with the world.

CHAPTER 2

Wednesday, December 16 – the week before Christmas

"Are you finished with your breakfast, Mr. Rockingham? We should be landing shortly."

"Yes, thank you." Ben nodded and the cabin attendant removed the tray. Their flight from Boston to London's Heathrow Airport had been smooth, but Ben was still glad to have finally arrived. He felt tired and a bit out of sorts.

Rob turned to him. "I'll be happy to get to the hotel. I didn't sleep much, and I'm feeling pretty beat right now. I'll be ready for a quick nap once we check in."

"Me too," Ben said. "I dozed for a while, but it was for less than two hours. A nap does sound really good."

"By the way," Rob told him, "the flight confirmation you gave me was only for this flight. Why isn't there a return

flight?"

"You'll need to ask Sam about that. She said something about a deal that was available, but you had to book the flights separately. I didn't understand it, but I gave her my credit card number and told her to do what she needed to do."

Rob eyed Ben curiously. "Hmmm. That sounds weird to me. Are you up to something, sweetheart?"

"I have no idea what you're talking about," Ben replied, his face a blank slate.

Rob was suspicious but didn't push. He'd corner Sam later and see if she was easier to read.

Once at the gate, the guys hurried to the baggage claim, then to customs. They were pleasantly surprised by how quickly they made it through before carrying on to the car rental counter. They'd debated whether or not to get a car now, as they'd only be in London for a couple of days and didn't expect to need one until they headed to the family home, known by everyone in the area as The Mews at Stoney Hill. The hotel assured them that they had a car park available, and getting the car now meant one less thing to do later.

Once the luggage was secured in the back of the SUV, Ben got behind the wheel. He navigated out of the airport and toward the M4, which would take them to Knightsbridge.

"You know where the hotel is, right?" Rob asked.

"I know the general area, but I put the address in my phone before we left. Can you pull it up in Maps, so we have exact directions, please? If traffic isn't bad, it should only take about a half hour to get there."

Rob grabbed Ben's phone from the console and unlocked it. Opening the Maps app, he started the directions to the hotel. For the next few days, they would be staying at the L17 Knightsbridge.

The hotel was just off Brompton Road, within walking distance to the world-famous Harrods, where Rob was planning to go shopping the next day. Traffic wasn't bad at all, and Ben pulled up in front of the hotel thirty-five minutes later. A doorman approached the vehicle and helped Rob with the luggage, directing Ben to the car park around the corner.

Once registered and in their room, they quickly decided that unpacking could wait. They stripped, Ben set an alarm on his phone, and they climbed into bed. They were both asleep within minutes.

BEN WOKE with Rob's lips wrapped around the head of his cock. "Mmmm. This is much better than waking to an alarm."

Nipping and licking up his body, Rob smiled. "I thought you might enjoy it." They kissed deeply; Ben grabbed Rob's ass and pulled him closer, his fingers sliding into Rob's crease, running the pad of his index finger over his pucker. Rob moaned, sucking on Ben's tongue. They separated, and Ben moved down and around so that they were mouth to cock.

Rob wasted no time licking and sucking the head of Ben's dick before tugging gently on his balls. Ben slicked his middle finger with spit, then slowly breached Rob's hole while his tongue circled Rob's crown, then dipped into the slit. Licking up and down Rob's length a few times, Ben took Rob's cock to the back of his throat, moving his finger deeper and stroking the bundle of nerves in Rob's channel.

Rob grunted and moved his mouth behind Ben's balls,

plunging his tongue into Ben's hole. After a few minutes, Ben felt Rob's finger slide in as Rob licked his balls, then slowly encircled the head of his cock.

They continued pleasuring each other for several minutes, slowing down then speeding up, teasing and edging the way they both loved so much.

Ben pulled off Rob's cock. "Please, I really need to come," he panted.

Rob redoubled his efforts, and Ben followed suit. Moments later, Ben's spunk hit the back of Rob's throat. He swallowed greedily as his own orgasm tore through him, and he came hard. They continued to lick and nip each other while their breathing returned to normal. Rob moved around to kiss Ben deeply. "I love you so much."

"And I love you, handsome," Ben replied quietly. "Some days, I still can't believe we found each other." Times like this reminded Ben how much his life had changed for the better. A year ago, he hadn't realized how much he missed being with someone. Then he met Rob, and his world turned upside down. He was so much happier now, and part of him knew that Rob felt the same way.

"Me neither. But we did, and it just keeps getting better. Now let's get cleaned up, so we can go get something to eat. It seems I've worked up an appetite."

THEY SAT at the hotel bar, discussing dining options and enjoying some wine. William, the bartender, had heard them talking about restaurants and suggested a few different places nearby. Finally, they'd decided on an Italian restaurant that was within walking distance.

"You're all set, sirs. You have an eight-thirty reservation at Scalini. Would you both like another glass of wine?"

"Sure," Ben replied. "That would be great, thank you."

As William was replenishing their glasses, Rob's phone rang. "It's Sam. I should take this."

The bar was a bit noisy, so he stepped away, moving to a quieter area between the bar and the hotel lobby.

"Hey, Sam. Is everything okay?"

"Hi, Rob. Sorry to bother you, but I have a huge favor to ask."

"Sure. What's wrong?"

"It's my cousin, Jon. I think I may have told you about him. He and my aunt got into a huge fight, and he showed up on my doorstep today. He really needs a break from her and her toxicity. Would it be okay if I brought him to England with me?"

"Of course! He's your family, Sam, so that makes him our family too. And yes, you've told me about him. From what I remember about comments you've made about your aunt, she *is* quite toxic about a lot of things—getting away from her for a while sounds like a good thing."

"Thank you," Sam said. "I really appreciate it. I'm pretty sure I can get Jon on my flight, but I'll let you know if anything changes."

"It's really last minute, Sam. If the flight is super-expensive, use the credit card of mine that you have on file."

"Thanks, sweetie. I appreciate that, but I think it'll be okay. I've still got a bunch of points with the airline, so I'm gonna try to use those if I can. Also, Matthew called me this morning, he dropped by the office and delivered the bracelets to me. Oh, Rob, they're absolutely gorgeous."

"Excellent," Rob said excitedly. "I knew he'd do a great job with them. I feel better that they're finished, and you have them. Now just don't forget them."

A year earlier, Rob had stopped wearing his wedding ring once he and Ben had figured out there was something between them. Part of his heart would always belong to Alan, but he didn't feel comfortable with the ring on his finger anymore. He'd been thinking about doing something with the ring to repurpose it but hadn't decided what that should be.

A few months after that, he had stopped into his friend Matthew's shop, the Artistic Alchemist, to talk with him about a piece of jewelry to give to Ben for Christmas. Matt had come up with an idea that solved both problems—a gift for Ben and a way to reuse Rob's wedding ring.

"Don't worry," Sam chided him. "I won't forget them. They're already in my carry-on bag. Relax. Okay, I'll let you go. Thanks again, give Ben a kiss for me. See you in a couple of days."

"Love you, Sam. See you soon."

"Is everything okay?" Ben asked when Rob returned to his seat at the bar.

"Yes and no. Sam's cousin Jon is going through a difficult time. I'm not sure of the details, but his mom can be quite cruel. He showed up at Sam's rather suddenly. She wanted to know if he could join us for Christmas; of course, I said yes."

"Okay. One more isn't a problem, and if he's having a bad time, it's better that he's with us."

Rob's heart warmed at the fact that Ben was always of the same mind as he was regarding things like this. Sam's cousin needed help, so he helped without question. Rob thanked his lucky stars that Ben was such a good man, and that they were starting to make a life together.

"I agree. Now let's finish up our wine and go to dinner. I'm hungry."

DINNER WAS DELICIOUS. They shared carpaccio with a tangy mustard dressing for an appetizer, then split a pasta course of tagliolini in a tomato sauce with onions and pancetta. For entrées, Rob selected salmon with prawns in a lemon and butter sauce while Ben opted for the branzino dressed with herbed olive oil and balsamic vinegar. Everything was cooked to perfection, and they lingered over cappuccinos while they talked about the rest of the trip.

"I want to go to Harrods tomorrow to do some last-minute shopping," Rob began. "Now that Jon is joining us, we should have something for him under the tree."

"Good idea. I'd also like to pick up something for the estate manager. We kind of sprang this on her at the last minute, so I'd like to show our appreciation. Did I tell you she arranged for someone to come in and handle Christmas dinner for us?" Ben asked. "That way everyone can relax and not have to worry about preparing a big meal."

Rob's face lit up. "Really? Oh, that's wonderful! I feel bad about someone else having to cook on Christmas Day, though. Do you know who it is? We can buy a gift for them as well."

"I'll call Sheila, the estate manager, tomorrow and get all the details, but I'm pretty sure it's an older lady from the village who has helped out our family in the past. She used to work as a domestic and has no real family in the area anymore. Apparently, she's happy to be doing something. I think the plan is to have her and a couple of other women come in and do most of the prep work during the day on Christmas Eve. Then she'll come back the next day to finish up. I told Sheila that we didn't need anything formal, and she said she'd take care of it."

"That sounds great," Rob said. "Once you get the details from Sheila tomorrow, we can figure out exactly what gifts we need to shop for at Harrods."

"I love how you immediately thought of picking up gifts for everyone," Ben replied. "My mom was the same way. In fact, she usually had a few extra gifts tucked away just in case someone unexpectedly showed up. The thought of someone not having a gift to open on Christmas morning would upset her terribly. You're a good man, Rob Asher."

"Wow, it's funny that you say that about your mom. Mine did exactly the same thing." Rob reached over and squeezed Ben's hand. "We were both raised by very caring women."

They linked arms as they walked back to the hotel. Rob once again thanked his lucky stars that Ben was part of his life.

CHAPTER 3

"Are you sure you want to go to Harrods? It's going to be a madhouse, you know." Ben knew he wouldn't get Rob to change his mind, but he tried one last time anyway. "I'm sure you can find whatever you need at other shops and definitely for less money." They were having breakfast at the hotel restaurant, and Ben wanted to make sure Rob was fully prepared for the craziness of shopping at Harrods the week before Christmas.

"I know, but I've never been, and I really want to see it—especially since it's Christmastime, and I'm sure the decorations will be amazing."

"Fine, just remember what I told you, there's no way you'll be able to see everything, so we need to have a plan, okay?" Ben had told Rob as much as he could about what Harrods was like, and they'd even watched a few YouTube videos, but he knew that Rob would be like a little kid when he actually walked through the doors.

"I get it, and I've thought a bit about what to get for gifts. I just need to know exactly how many people I'm buying for." Rob paused, squinting his eyes in thought. "I think a scarf would be nice for Jon. Maybe some chocolates too. And for the ladies who are coming in to cook for us, some candy or biscuits and perhaps a selection of tea. That should narrow down where we need to go in the store. I know you said that there are boxes of Christmas decorations at the house, but I want to pick up a few new ornaments. We can use them this year and then take them home as souvenirs."

"Great. When we get back to our room, I'll call Sheila and ask her how many women will be helping with dinner. Then we can head out. The sooner we get there the faster we'll be done."

THEY AMBLED DOWN THE STREET, pausing to look at several of the window displays before they reached the entrance to Harrods. Rob felt like a child experiencing Christmas for the very first time. "Oh my God, this is so cool! I can't believe I'm really here."

As they entered the store, Rob's jaw hung open, and his eyes bulged. "I have no words." Rob turned to Ben and saw him smiling. "What? I've never seen anything like this before. It's amazing!" The Christmas decorations were stunning. Evergreen garlands festooned every surface with glistening gold ornaments, tiny white lights, and deep burgundy ribbons. It truly was magical.

"I know, sweetheart. I love how enthralled you are by it all. But it's just going to get crazier as the morning progresses. Let's head up to the men's department first and see if we can find a scarf for Jon," Ben suggested, pulling Rob along toward the escalators. "Then we can head to the food hall."

Rob followed Ben's lead, his head swiveling, trying to take it all in. "We need to come back here sometime when it's not Christmas. Can we do that?"

"Of course we can, sweetheart. But for now, you need to focus."

After a few minutes, they reached the men's department and located the section with scarves on display. After looking through several options, Rob found a cashmere scarf in a navy and pale gray plaid with a bit of bright orange in the weave. The label indicated it was from British designer Paul Smith. "I think I'll get this one for Jon." It wasn't too busy yet, so they quickly located a salesman who boxed up the scarf and completed the sale. Ben asked for directions to the food hall and off they went. It took a while to get there, but they were able to weave their way through the ever-growing crowds in the various departments they passed.

As they reached the food hall, Ben pulled Rob aside. "We'll need gifts for the four ladies who will be helping to prepare dinner. That includes Mrs. Harrison, who'll be there on Christmas Day. She's the woman I remember. She helped out a few times when my parents were still living there and decided to throw a large party. She's also helped get things ready a few times when either Mike and Ellen or Kyle and I were there for a visit. If I remember correctly, she enjoys a glass of sherry now and then, so I may get a bottle for her. Then there's Sheila and also a cleaning woman who will come in and tidy up for us while we're all there."

Ben paused, taking a breath. He appeared to be counting things in his head. "That's a total of six women we need something for. And there's Mr. Dobbins, a gentleman from town who is available if anything needs fixing during our stay. I thought we could pick up a bottle of whisky for him."

"Okay," replied Rob. "For most of the women, it might be easier if we get multiples of things. Let me see what they have for tea assortments." He scanned the area and saw some choices on a nearby display. Next, he spotted a counter with a wide variety of macaroons and decided to get some of those. He had to wait a few minutes until someone was available to help him, then asked for six boxes of the assorted specialty cookies.

"A dozen in each box. Choose whatever you'd like and make an interesting mix in each box, please," he told the salesperson. When she was finished, he handed her the tea selections that Ben had been holding for him.

She rang up the sale and said to Rob, "If you're doing more shopping, sir, I can have this all sent to Customer Collections for you. When you're ready to leave, you can stop by and pick everything up. That way you don't have to carry everything around with you."

"That would be wonderful. Thank you."

Once Rob was finished, Ben turned to him. "Why don't we head down to wines and spirits and pick up a few things there? Then we can grab a bite to eat."

"Sounds like a plan."

After choosing a few bottles of wine, a bottle of sherry for

Mrs. Harrison, and a nice bottle of whisky, Ben asked for those to be sent to Customer Collections as well. They made their way to the second floor for a well-deserved lunch at Pizzeria & Pasqua.

Rob sighed as he sipped his Prosecco. "We got a lot done, although we have been at it for over three hours already. I know you said it would be busy here, but somehow I wasn't expecting it to be this crazy." As excited as he was to actually be *in* Harrods, Rob was rather exhausted at this point, so he relished the time sitting and drinking his wine.

Ben chuckled. "You need to understand that Harrods is a tourist destination as well as a department store. Plus, a lot of the people who live in this area are quite well-off, and this is where they normally shop. While Harrods attracts tourists all year long, it's especially busy at Christmastime."

"Fair enough. As busy as it is, I'm still glad we came. After lunch, I'd like to see about picking up an ornament or two, and then we can head back to the hotel."

After enjoying their salads and wood-fired prosciutto and mushroom pizza, they braved the crowds again and eventually located the section of the store dedicated to Christmas decor. Rob found a silver ornament of the London skyline that he thought Jon might like and picked one up for Sam as well. He noticed one that was the facade of the Harrods store and thought that would be a perfect souvenir for Ben and him. There was quite a line to make his purchase, but he waited patiently. When he was finally done, they headed to Customer Collections to retrieve the rest of their purchases.

As they left Customer Collections with their bags and boxes, an employee dressed all in green offered to help them carry their purchases out.

"They're affectionately called the Green Men," Ben explained. "They act as customer service ambassadors and help in any way they can."

"Shall I hail a taxi for you?" The Green Man asked as they exited the store.

"Yes, please," replied Ben. The hotel wasn't far, but a taxi would be easier than walking with so many packages. Once safely in the cab, Ben gave the driver the address of the hotel, and they were off.

CHAPTER 4

Thursday, December 17 – the week before Christmas

The day was clear and sunny and thankfully not very cold, so once they got all their packages safely back to their hotel room, Ben and Rob decided to take a walk through the neighborhood. They wandered a bit, not overly concerned about exactly where they were going. Ben was familiar with the area, so he kept them from getting lost or straying too far from their hotel.

"You're awfully quiet, Ben. Is everything okay?"

"Yeah, everything's fine. I've just been thinking about the whole thing with Mike. I still don't understand why he didn't seem excited about coming to England for Christmas this year." Ben paused thoughtfully, then went on. "I just don't get it. Even when I called him the week after Thanksgiving, he was blatantly evasive. I think Kyle may have talked to him, but I'm not sure he learned anything either."

Rob put his arm around Ben's shoulders and squeezed lightly. "Maybe you can find some time to talk to him once he and Ellen arrive. I'd hate to think that there's some rift between you, especially at this time of year."

"Yeah, I definitely want to speak with him. If something's going on, I want to help. Now not to change the subject, but do we need to get anything else before we head to the house?" Ben asked.

"No, I don't think so," Rob replied. "There are places to shop in the village, right? We do have a car, so we can head to a larger town or city if we need something. We'll be fine."

"Okay. Sheila did say that someone was going to stock the essentials—bread, butter, milk, coffee, things like that, and a few things for potential meals; she asked what foods we like, so I made up a list for her. There's a bakery and a butcher in the village, along with a post office, so we can get pretty much anything we'd need."

Rob seemed confused. "Post office? I don't think we'll have a big need for stamps or anything, but I could be wrong."

"Oh, sorry. Post offices in the towns and villages here double as small convenience stores," Ben told him. "They carry a small selection of groceries, beer, wine, and liquor. In addition to the normal post office duties, of course."

"Ah, that makes sense now. Thanks for explaining." Rob chuckled. "I couldn't understand why you thought stamps were essential."

They walked in companionable silence for a few minutes, taking in the sights and enjoying the sunshine. In the next block, Ben stopped and pointed to a pub on the corner. "Care for a pint?"

"Sure. Lead the way."

The pub wasn't overly crowded yet, so Rob grabbed a table in the corner while Ben went to the bar for their beers. Rob looked around, taking in the dark green walls and gleaming oak wainscoting as well as the brass wall sconces that gave the room a golden glow. It seemed like the perfect spot for a late afternoon break.

A few minutes later, Ben returned with two glasses. "A Seriously Bad Elf for you and a Tangle Foot for me." He placed the pints on the table and sat next to Rob, so they could both people-watch.

"Excuse me, 'Seriously Bad Elf'? What the hell is that?" Rob exclaimed.

"Sorry," Ben said. "The British often come up with weird names for beer, and since it's Christmastime, there are some holiday choices right now. That one is a sweet ale with a bit of citrus, from what I was told."

"Oh, that's tasty," Rob said after cautiously taking his first sip. "Good choice despite the name."

"I figured you'd like it. They have something called a Ginger Beard that I thought you might enjoy as well. According to the barman, it's got a spicy ginger flavor. And this Tangle Foot is a light ale with hints of butter and honey."

"Hmmm, I may need to try the Ginger Beard next." Rob winked, loving that Ben knew him so well.

"Might as well. The hotel's not far, and we can probably get a bite to eat here if you want. We've got nowhere to be, so relaxing and enjoying a night at a pub sounds like a plan to me."

The door to the bar opened, and a very tall blond man walked in. He scanned the area and then zeroed in on Ben and Rob. Walking toward them purposefully, he said, "Ben? Is that you?"

"Alex? Oh my God, I don't believe it!"

Ben stood and wrapped the man in a strong hug.

Rob watched them and felt a twinge of something uncomfortable. Was he jealous? He didn't think so, but there was obviously some history between the two men.

Finally separating, Ben looked at Rob. "Rob, this is Alex Whiteshaw. He and I went to secondary school together. That would be high school for you." Turning to Alex, he continued, "Alex, this is Rob Asher, my boyfriend."

Rob stood, offering his hand. "Very nice to meet you."

"Likewise," Alex replied. "I saw the Instagram post of the both of you last year. I didn't realize that our Ben here fancied boys. Had I known back at school, I may have tried to make a move on him."

His tone was light; Rob sensed that there was nothing but some fun flirtation in his words.

"Honestly, Alex," Ben interrupted, "I don't think I knew who I fancied back then. I didn't have my first boyfriend until college back in the States, and even then, I wasn't really sure about myself. Meeting Rob last year was pretty life-changing for me."

"As long as you're happy, mate. That's all that matters," Alex said. "And just to be clear, I'm very happy for both of you." His smile reached his eyes, and Rob could sense the honesty in his words.

"Thanks, Alex. I have to agree with Ben. I didn't think I'd ever find love again, but a chance meeting last year changed all of that." Rob reached for Ben's hand and squeezed it tightly.

Ben smiled warmly at Rob, then his gaze shifted to Alex. "What about you, my friend? Anyone special in your life?"

"Not at the moment, but that doesn't mean I'm not looking. I've had a few relationships, but nothing's stuck yet." Alex chuckled. "I'm not giving up, though."

"Would you like to join us for a drink?" Rob asked.

"I'm meeting someone," Alex replied. "But I'm early, so yeah, I'd like that."

Ben chimed in. "Sit and I'll get it. What do you want?"

"Thanks, mate. I'll take a lager, please."

Alex sat and turned to Rob. "So what brings you two to London?"

"We're spending Christmas at Ben's family home in Stoney Hill. His son Kyle and his brother and sister-in-law, along with a few of our friends, are all going to be there. We decided to come to London for a couple of days first, but we're heading to the house tomorrow afternoon."

"Oh, nice. I've been to The Mews a couple of times when we were on holiday at school. I didn't realize that the family still had the home. It's a beautiful place."

"Yeah, the house was left to Ben and Mike when their mom passed away. This will be my first time going there, but Ben and Kyle have spent a few vacations there over the years. It's gonna be nice to have some of the family together for the holidays."

Ben returned with Alex's beer. "So Alex, how have you been? I can't remember the last time we talked."

"It's been years, for sure. I'm working for an advertising agency here in London. I've been here for about six years now.

I was at a smaller agency in Liverpool before that, but I missed London a lot. Eventually, I got this opportunity and I'm glad I made the move."

"That's great," Ben said.

Alex nodded, then sipped his beer and continued, "Rob tells me you're headed to The Mews for Christmas. I'm quite happy you kept the family home. It's a lovely place, and I have fond memories of staying there."

"Yeah, I can't imagine not having it in the family. Life gets in the way sometimes, but I try to get back whenever I can. I have lots of good memories of the place too." Ben paused, and Rob noticed a thoughtful look on his face. Ben smiled briefly at Rob and pushed on. "Do you have plans for Christmas, Alex? You're welcome to join us if you'd like."

"Thanks anyway, but I do have plans on Christmas Day. Spending time with Mum and my sister Penny and her family up in Derby."

"Excellent. How is the fam?" Ben asked Alex.

"Mum's doing okay although she's getting on. She lives with Penny and her husband now. They're all doing well, and I try to get up to visit them often."

"Please tell them I said hello and merry Christmas. Oh, what about Boxing Day? You could come down and visit then, right? I know Mike would love to see you."

"That I can do. It will be great to see him again."

Just then, a handsome dark-haired man approached their table and placed his hand on Alex's shoulder.

"Oh hey, Jeremy." Alex stood and gave the man a peck on the cheek. "Jeremy, this is Ben and his boyfriend, Rob."

"Oh my goodness," the guy said, eyes widening. "You're Ben Rockingham, aren't you? It's very nice to meet you both."

As they shook hands, Alex joked, "Ben and I were at secondary school together a hundred years ago."

Alex checked his watch, then turned to Jeremy. "I didn't realize the time. Sorry, but we've got a reservation to keep. Ben, it was great seeing you again and so nice to meet you, Rob. I'll see you on Boxing Day. Um, what time?"

"Come for lunch, please. It was great seeing you again." Ben handed him a card. "Here's my cell number. Call if you get lost or change your mind."

"Will do, mate. Cheers."

After Alex and Jeremy left, Rob turned to Ben. "He seems very nice. I'm glad we ran into him."

"Me too. He was a good friend, but over the years we lost touch. I hope he shows up at the house next week."

Rob drained his glass. "Okay, I think I'd like to try the Ginger Beard and have some dinner. Is there a menu?"

Ben chuckled, standing up. "I'll get right on that."

CHAPTER 5

After a nice leisurely breakfast in the hotel's restaurant, Rob and Ben decided to take a walk before heading out to Stoney Hill. The day was a bit cool, but they enjoyed the crisp air and kept a steady pace to keep warm. It was only a couple of hours to the house, so if they left around lunch time, they'd still arrive by mid-afternoon. Sam, Jon, Kyle, and Julie would be flying in the next day, and Ben wanted to be sure everything was ready at the house when they arrived.

"What time did you say they were getting in tomorrow?" Ben asked as they meandered through the neighborhood.

"Sam and Jon land around eleven in the morning, and Kyle gets in shortly after them. If I remember correctly, Julie doesn't arrive until around one o'clock, but they're all going to wait for her. They've rented an SUV for the four of them," Rob said. "If there aren't any delays and even if they stop for lunch or something, they'll be at the house before dinner."

"Okay, good. Sheila said she'd stop by this afternoon to make sure everything's in order—I'm sure it will be—but she always likes to see for herself. She's got food scheduled to be delivered this morning, and Mrs. Harrison will be there to get it all put away. The cleaning lady was in earlier this week to give the place a thorough going over—washing and dusting, fresh linens on the beds."

"Wow, you've taken care of everything. Do we need to stop and get liquor?"

"No, Sheila took care of that as well. She asked me for a list of what we normally drink and said she'd arrange for delivery. I'm guessing that's being delivered today too. And we can always pick up stuff in Stoney Hill if we should happen to run out."

Before they knew it, an hour had flown by. Ben had once again kept them in the general vicinity of the hotel, leading them up and down various streets for a few blocks before turning the other way.

"Did you want to have some lunch before we leave the city or stop somewhere along the way? We've got time; we could make a detour to Winchester on the way. There are quite a few pubs there where we can get lunch. The trip will be a bit longer, but we really don't have any place to be. I can text Sheila and tell her we probably won't get to the house until later this afternoon."

"Winchester for lunch sounds like a great idea," Rob agreed. "I want to see as much of the area as I can while we're here."

Once back at the hotel, they packed up the car, and with Ben behind the wheel and the Maps app guiding them, they were on their way.

ONCE OUT OF LONDON, the drive turned pleasant, and the time passed quickly. The scenery was varied along the way, but Rob found it all beautiful and so different from what he normally saw in the States. They soon arrived in Winchester, where Ben found a car park without too much trouble. After a short walk, they arrived at a pub called The Bishop on the Bridge. It wasn't overly crowded; they were able to get a table near some windows that overlooked the water.

Ben ordered a pint of Fuller's London Pride while Rob opted for Fuller's Frontier. After perusing the menu, Ben chose a burger, and Rob decided on fish and chips with mushy peas. The chips were advertised as triple cooked; they were very crispy and quite delicious. It was all very good indeed. Rob even liked the mushy peas, although Ben admitted that he wasn't overly fond of them.

It was just after three o'clock when they left the pub, enjoying a leisurely stroll back to the car park. The brisk air refreshed them for the last leg of their journey which, according to Ben, would be just under an hour.

"It's really beautiful here," Rob said when they exited the car park. "Do you think we'll have time to come back while we're here? I'd like to visit the cathedral."

"We probably will. Some of the others may want to do some sightseeing too. There's quite a bit to see. Stonehenge isn't too far from the house, and the Port of Southampton is pretty close as well."

"Cool. I've been to Stonehenge before. Alan and I went there one year before a cruise from Southampton. We can talk it over with the gang and maybe plan a couple of day trips."

Before they knew it, they'd reached the village of Stoney Hill, and Ben pointed out the main square with a small park in the center. "There's a sports field at the other end of the park. Mike and I use to play a bit of football there when we were younger." Ben smiled at the memory.

They drove along the main road, passing a pub, a bakery, the post office, and butcher shop, along with a few other small storefronts.

"This is charming!" Rob exclaimed. "I had no idea it would be so quaint. I love it."

"It is very nice and hasn't really changed much over the years. It gets a bit of tourist traffic in the spring and summer, but it's pretty quiet here right now. And the house is close enough, so it's an easy walk into town."

Ben steered the car onto a small road at the edge of town, and after a short drive alongside an ancient stone wall, they turned into an opening in the wall. It was, in fact, a tree-lined driveway with large wrought iron gates that were opened as if welcoming them in.

"We keep the gates closed when no one's here. Sheila must have come by this morning to open them for the deliveries."

Up ahead on the right, Rob saw a gorgeous two-story house of tan stone. "Oh my goodness, your home is beautiful," he said, clearly in awe. "You've shown me photos of The Mews, but it seems so much grander in real life."

Beyond the house, there were fields separated by low stone walls and stands of trees, along with rolling hills in the distance. It was remarkably picturesque and exactly what he thought of as the English countryside.

There were two cars parked to the right of the front door, so Ben pulled the SUV into a spot to the left of the entrance.

Pointing toward the vehicles, Ben said, "It looks like Sheila and Mrs. Harrison are here. Let's go in, and I'll introduce you. We can unload the car later."

Walking in the front door, Rob found himself in a bright and airy foyer. An ornate wooden staircase led to the second floor, with open doorways on both sides leading to what appeared to be sitting rooms. Ben started down a hallway at the back of the foyer, and Rob followed him.

"Where are we going?"

"The kitchen. That's probably where everyone is."

At that moment, a woman entered the hallway from a doorway on the left.

"I thought I heard voices. Ben!" she exclaimed. "Welcome back."

"Hi, Sheila. Thanks!"

She was of average height and had soft brown hair cut in a fashionable bob.

Ben grinned at her. "Sheila, I'd like you to meet my boyfriend, Rob Asher."

"It's so nice to finally meet you, Rob." Sheila smiled warmly.

"Likewise," Rob replied. "Ben speaks very highly of you."

"Thanks. I've managed the property for Ben and his family for many years. I'm happy to say that we've grown to be rather good friends," Sheila replied. "Let's go into the kitchen. Mrs. Harrison is just finishing up."

Rob and Ben followed Sheila through the same doorway that she'd appeared from. The kitchen was large and bright, with modern stainless steel appliances and a large island with seating along one side. In the corner near a large set of windows was a round table with four chairs, as well as two upholstered wing chairs off to the side. Washing a few dishes at the sink was an older woman with short white hair. As she turned and smiled, Rob noticed her striking blue eyes. At first glance, she reminded him of Dame Judi Dench.

"Mr. Rockingham! So good to see you again." The woman dried her hands and gave Ben a hug. "It's been too long."

"That it has, Mrs. Harrison. And please, call me Ben."

"Only if you call me Ethel," she said, eyes sparkling with amusement.

"We know that's not gonna happen, Mrs. H. But you used to call me Master Ben when I was younger."

"That was when your parents were still here, God rest their souls. Now you and your brother are lords of the manor, as it were."

Changing the subject, Ben said, "Mrs. H, I'd like you to meet Rob Asher, my boyfriend."

Rob extended his hand. "I'm pleased to—"

"None of that now." She drew him into a hug. "You're family. It's very nice to meet you, Master Rob." There was a twinkle in her eye as if she had purposely called him that just to give Ben a hard time.

"But, but ..." Ben stammered. "Why?"

"It's so easy to tease him," Mrs. H said to Rob, smirking knowingly. "You'd think he'd have learned by now." She turned to Ben. "So, Master Ben," she continued, "when are Master Kyle and the rest arriving?"

"Kyle and my assistant, Julie, arrive on Sunday along with Rob's best friend Samantha and her cousin, Jon. Mike and Ellen will be here on Monday."

"What about young Mike?" She asked, inquiring about Ben's nephew.

"No, Mike Jr. and his wife just had a baby a few months ago, and he hasn't been in his present job very long, so they're staying home this year," Ben said. "But I'm sure we'll have a video call with them on Christmas Day."

"Lovely. It's nice that some of the family is getting together here for Christmas, though. It's been too long since that happened." Mrs. H checked her watch and patted Ben's shoulder. "Well, I must be off. I wasn't sure if you'd feel like cooking much tonight, so I made a cottage pie for your dinner. It's in the fridge. Just put it in a moderate oven for about forty-five minutes. And I baked some scones too. Those will be nice with elevenses or afternoon tea." She pointed to a glass-dome-covered cake plate on the island.

"Thank you so much, Mrs. Harrison," Rob said. "You needn't have gone to so much trouble, but we do appreciate it."

"Yes, thank you, Mrs. H," Ben added. "That was very kind of you."

Mrs. Harrison nodded with a smile. "No trouble at all. I'll be back on Christmas Eve with a few other ladies, and we'll get everything ready for your Christmas dinner. If you need anything else in the meantime, my number is by the phone."

She hugged them goodbye and was off.

Sheila turned to Ben and Rob. "Groceries and liquor

arrived this morning, and Mrs. H put all the food away. I stored the liquor behind the bar in the family room. Before I forget, a Christmas tree and some flower arrangements will be delivered on Monday morning."

Sheila paused as if going through a mental checklist. "I did a walk-through of the house before you arrived. Everything's been cleaned, and there are fresh linens on all the beds. The upstairs rooms were a bit stuffy, so I opened a few windows just a little to circulate the air. I should close those before I head out."

"We can take care of that, Sheila," Ben said. "I need to give Rob a tour anyway. Thanks for everything."

"Of course. Call me if you need anything. It's great seeing you again, Ben, and so nice to finally meet you, Rob. Tell the rest of the fam I said hello."

"Will do. Thanks again, Sheila. If you're not doing anything, why don't you stop by on Boxing Day? We ran into a schoolmate of mine while we were in London; he's supposed to be here around lunchtime."

"Thanks. I'd like that."

After Sheila left, Ben gave Rob a quick tour of the house, and as promised to Sheila, they shut the upstairs windows. The downstairs had a small formal sitting room, dining room, and kitchen on one side, and a large family room and office on the other. There was also a half-bath tucked behind the foyer. Upstairs featured six bedrooms and four bathrooms, along with a laundry room and a small sitting area. Ben had left the master bedroom for Mike and Ellen, as it was quite grand and had an en suite bathroom. He and Rob chose the larger guest room, which also had its own bath. The rest of the group would use the remaining four bedrooms with two adjoining bathrooms. After the tour, they got everything out of the car and unpacked.

After finishing in their room, the guys went back downstairs. Rob turned on the oven for dinner, and Ben found a bottle of malbec at the bar in the family room. While they waited for the cottage pie to heat up, Ben opened the wine, and they sat in club chairs in front of a window near the fireplace.

"How does it feel to be home?" Rob asked. He knew that the past year had been a busy one, and Ben had really been looking forward to coming here.

"It feels good—right. I missed this place so much. I always feel more centered when I'm here, although I must admit, your house is a close second. It definitely feels like home too."

"I'm glad. I want you to feel comfortable there. You know you can spend as much time at my place as you want, right?"

"I do. And that makes me really happy," Ben admitted. "In fact, how would you feel about my spending even more time there?"

"I'd love that." Rob's heart swelled. He'd been wanting to spend more time with Ben but hadn't broached the subject of them living together yet. Part of him was afraid that Ben might think it was too soon, although this conversation was making him extremely hopeful. "But don't you want to spend time in Los Angeles? Amanda and Julie are both there and you are an actor after all. Doesn't it make more sense for you to be based in LA?"

"With the play I did this year, I spent more time in New York and at your house than I did in LA. With internet and video calls, I can work with Julie and Amanda without actually being there. I've been thinking about maybe selling my house there since it seems to be a waste. If I do need to go to LA once in a while, I can stay at a hotel."

"So you wanna move in with me, Ben? I'm completely on board with that."

"Yeah, I'd like that a lot."

***

THEY MADE LOVE SLOWLY, neither of them in any rush for it to end. Rob teased at Ben's nipples, first one, then the other, coaxing them into firm buds that he licked and lightly nipped. As Ben moaned, Rob moved lower, kissing down Ben's hairy chest and stomach, licking at the trail of dark hair that ended in a neatly trimmed patch just above his leaking cock.

Rob swiped his tongue across the head, gathering up the precum and savoring its bittersweetness. Taking Ben all the way to the back of his throat, he heard Ben moan again as Rob hollowed his cheeks and continued slowly moving up and down his length.

He paused to wet his finger, then went back to gently sucking the head of Ben's dick as he reached behind his balls and circled his hole. He pressed in slowly as he lapped and nipped at the crown of Ben's cock.

Rob could hear Ben panting and knew he was trying to hold off a bit longer, but Rob had something else in mind. Lifting Ben's legs, he drove his tongue into Ben's pucker over and over.

"Oh God, that's so good!" Ben exclaimed.

"Do you want my cock inside you, sweetie?" Rob teased.

"Please!" Ben pleaded.

Reaching for the lube on the nightstand, Rob coated his

fingers and worked them into Ben. Once Ben was fully prepped, Rob moved forward and lined up the head of his stiff cock against Ben's hole. He breached Ben and paused, relishing the tight heat surrounding the tip of his dick, then pushed ahead slowly until his balls rested on Ben's ass. He leaned forward and took Ben's mouth in a smoldering kiss.

Breaking the kiss, Ben whispered, "Move, please move."

Rob began slow and steady thrusts, pulling almost all the way out and then plunging back in. Picking up speed, he grabbed Ben's rigid cock in his hand and began to jerk him in time with his thrusts.

"Come with me," he panted. He could feel Ben's balls pull up and knew they were both close. Ben tugged him closer for another searing kiss as he felt Ben spill over his hand. Ben's channel tightened around him; Rob came so hard his vision clouded. They breathed heavily, breath ghosting over each other's mouths as they sought another kiss.

"I love you so much," Rob whispered into Ben's ear. "So damn much."

"And I love you."

Neither wanted to move from the comfort of the other's arms, but Rob knew they'd be stuck together and uncomfortable if they stayed like that too long. He rose and went into the bathroom, returning with a warm, wet washcloth and towel to clean them up.

Kissing once more, they fell asleep hugging tightly.

CHAPTER 6

Saturday, December 19 – at The Mews

Ben's bladder woke him just after seven o'clock, and he knew he wouldn't get back to sleep. After taking care of business in the bathroom, he pulled on a pair of flannel sleep pants and a sweatshirt, grabbed his Kindle and phone, and headed to the kitchen to make coffee.

He poured himself a mug, then sat in a comfy chair by the kitchen window to check his emails. Since nothing seemed to vitally need his attention, he relaxed and opened his Kindle to enjoy a quiet morning read.

Once he'd drained his first heavenly cup of caffeine and was pouring a second one, Ben noticed the stacked fruit bowl on the island. He remembered seeing some strawberries and blueberries in the fridge, so he decided to make a delicious fruit salad for breakfast. He remembered Mrs. H suggesting the scones for afternoon tea or elevenses but knew that Rob would enjoy one of the baked goods with the fruit.

Just as he finished chopping the fruit, Rob entered the kitchen, still looking half asleep and adorable.

"Good morning, sunshine," Ben said, giving Rob a quick kiss on the mouth before pouring him some coffee.

"G'morning and bless you," Rob mumbled as he accepted the steaming brew. Clearly, he was trying to wake up but wasn't being too successful. He inhaled deeply, bliss showing clearly on his face as the aroma hit him. "I woke up to an empty bed, and you know I really don't like that."

"I know, but I couldn't sleep, so I came downstairs, so I wouldn't disturb you. Sit and drink your coffee, and let it do its magic. I just made a fruit salad that we can have with the scones. Do you want some yogurt too?"

"Yes, please, but in about ten minutes. I need to wait for the caffeine to kick in."

Ben chuckled and sat back down. They sipped their coffee in pleasant silence while Rob looked out the window at the bright cerulean sky, and Ben read a bit more.

Finishing his first cup, Rob got up to get a refill and top off Ben's cup too. Ben returned the favor by serving them both yogurt along with some jam and clotted cream to go with the scones. They sat elbow to elbow, enjoying their breakfast and each other's company.

"Did you want to do anything special today?" Rob asked after they'd eaten their fill.

"It looks like a beautiful day; I was thinking we could take a walk into town. It'll be brisk, but we can handle it." Ben smiled at the thought of showing Rob the area up close. He reached over and took Rob's hand. "I can point out the sights, and we can stop at the pub for lunch if you'd like."

"That sounds like a great idea."

In short order, they tidied up the kitchen and went upstairs to shower and dress.

It was a crisp eight degrees out—about 46 degrees Fahrenheit, thanks to the Converter app on Rob's phone—but the sun was shining, and the sky was a brilliant blue with a few puffy clouds floating by. They'd dressed warmly and enjoyed their walk into the center of Stoney Hill.

There were quite a few people strolling about, and several nodded or said hello as if they recognized Ben, but knowing he was famous, didn't want to intrude. The townspeople were always so considerate; Ben appreciated the gesture. They both returned the greetings, and Ben visibly relaxed a bit more. Coming here always made him feel like he belonged.

They took their time ambling through the small park in the middle of town, eventually stopping to relax on a wooden bench to take in the sights. Ben pointed out a few of the shops along the main street and where folks sat at tables in the bakery window enjoying a cup of coffee or tea and probably the latest gossip.

"I can see why you like it here so much," Rob said. "It's charming."

"I'm glad you like it," Ben said. "We'll need to make plans to come back when the weather's warmer. It's gorgeous in the springtime when everything is in bloom."

"We talked about a cruise in the spring. I'll ask Sam to see what's available in April. Maybe we could sail from New York to Southampton, then spend a week here. Do you think that would work?" Rob asked.

"Yes, I'd love that. I know Sam's on vacation, but we should ask her this week, so we don't forget. I like having something to look forward to with you."

Rob pulled out his phone and typed something. "Okay, I made myself a note to ask her about it in the next few days."

"Excellent. Let's walk a bit more and work up an appetite for lunch."

They walked hand in hand to the far end of the park, then meandered through a small neighborhood there, just taking it easy and spending time together. They worked their way back to the main street and entered the Plough and Scythe Pub. It was warm and inviting, with lots of golden wood and cream walls.

Ben immediately recognized the older gentleman standing behind the bar. The man was wiping his hands on a white cloth and gazed toward the door when they entered. "Look what the cat dragged in! Welcome back, Ben. Sheila said you'd be here for Christmas."

Ben smiled warmly. "Hello, Carl. So nice to see you again. Carl, this is Rob Asher. Rob, Carl Ainsley."

"Ah, the infamous boyfriend," Carl teased, a twinkle in his eye. "Made quite a stir when you announced that last year, Ben. Very nice to meet you, Rob." Carl reached across the bar to shake Rob's hand. "I hope the press didn't give you too much shite over that."

"Nothing we couldn't handle, Carl," Ben said.

"All in all, it's been much better than we expected," Rob added.

"Good, fuck 'em if they've got a problem with it. It's none of their business. Now what can I get you? A pint of the local?"

Rob stared at Carl, speechless at the show of support for Ben.

"Yes, please. And some lunch, perhaps?" Ben added.

"Sure. You can take a table if you'd like, or the bar's fine too. We've got a ploughman's lunch, of course, steak and kidney pie, and Scotch eggs. Not as much as we usually have in the summer, but it's just a few of the regulars that come in this time of year."

"No problem at all. We don't need anything more than that, Carl."

They sat at the bar, and Carl brought over their beer. There was one man sitting at the end of the bar and two more at a table near the fireplace, but otherwise the bar was empty.

'Thank you for the support, Carl," Rob finally said. "That means a lot to us."

Ben smiled at Carl but spoke to Rob. "Carl's youngest, Billy, came out just before he left for university a few years ago. Kyle and I were here that summer for a few weeks. There was a bit of grumbling by some of the townsfolk, but Carl made sure folks understood that he and his family supported Billy and wouldn't tolerate any crap from anyone."

"Damn right, mate. No one's feckin' business who someone loves. People better leave that hate shite at the door, or I ask 'em not so kindly to leave."

"How's he doing?" Ben inquired. He sighed, thinking of all the good memories he had of his years growing up here and then later coming back with Kyle for visits. He realized that he thought of the people here as part of his extended family and was happy he could share some of that with Rob now.

"Good, thanks. He's settled down a bit. Uni's been good for him, and he's been seeing someone called Harry for a while now. Brought him home for a visit over the summer. I think he might stick around for a while." Carl paused, pride visible on his face. "He's coming here Christmas morning with Harry, and they'll stay through the weekend, so you may get to see him. And how's your fam doing?"

"They're all doing well. Kyle will be here tomorrow along with a few friends, and Mike and Ellen are arriving on Monday. I'm sure they'll all be by at some point."

"Great! I look forward to seeing them again. Now, what about some food?"

"I think I'll have the ploughman's lunch, please," Rob said.

"Good choice. We've got some cheese just in from Bailey's farm down the road and some fresh sausages that my wife Sarah made. Plus some pickled veggies that she put up this past summer."

"Sounds wonderful," Ben said, torn. "I was gonna go for the steak and kidney pie, but now I'm tempted to get the ploughman's too."

"Tell ya what—how 'bout I split a pie and the plough-man's? That way you can both share?" Carl winked.

"That sounds great. Thanks."

Carl headed into the kitchen and returned a few minutes later with two heaping plates of food. Each one had half an individual steak and kidney pie, a wedge of creamy white cheese, slices of sausage, some pickled beets, onions and carrots, a small dish of chutney, a sliced apple, and a couple of slices of whole-grain bread.

"Enjoy, gentlemen." He placed the plates in front of them and pulled out napkins and utensils from under the bar.

"Oh my God, this looks amazing!" Rob exclaimed.

"It does," Ben agreed. "Two more pints when you have a moment, please, Carl."

FOLLOWING THEIR FANTASTIC LUNCH, they wandered a bit more, hoping the exercise would help cancel out the food and drink they'd just consumed. When they finally returned home, Ben led Rob to the old carriage house on the property, explaining that it now served mainly as a garage and storage space, but that there was also a small apartment on the second floor.

After a bit of rummaging, Ben located several boxes marked "XMAS." It took a couple of trips to get them into the house but sorting through them made the task worthwhile. Among other things, there was a stand for the tree as well as lights and ornaments. Ben thought it might be fun to have a tree-decorating party one evening once they were all together.

"Some of these things are from when my parents still lived here," Ben said as he reviewed the contents of the boxes. "But the lights and a few of the ornaments are newer. I bought them when Kyle and I spent Christmas here several years back."

Rob unearthed a large box of battery-operated candles that could be set on a timer. "I'm going to put candles in the windows if that's okay."

"Absolutely. I think there should be enough for each window. Mum always loved candles in the windows for the holidays." Ben smiled at the memory. "We may need to get new batteries, but we can check them later. There's a Tesco Superstore in Amesbury. I can text Kyle, so that he and the others can stop there tomorrow and pick them up for us. It's on the way, so it shouldn't be a problem."

"Great idea. Let's put everything except the stand and the candles in the sitting room since we don't need that stuff yet. We can set up the stand in the corner of the family room, so that it's ready when the tree gets here on Monday. Then you and I can test the batteries and make a list of what we need."

Ben chuckled at Rob's rambling excitement. "I love it when you get bossy."

"Oh, do you? Well then, can you make me a drink? I'm all parched from being bossy." Rob smiled and gave Ben a peck on the cheek.

"Certainly, my love. I'll grab some ice in the kitchen and meet you in the family room."

Drinks made, they set to work checking the batteries and savoring their time together.

CHAPTER 7

Sunday, December 20 – at The Mews

"Remind me again of everyone's schedule today, please." Ben was seated at the kitchen island, sipping his coffee. They'd finished breakfast, and Ben was catching up on news on his phone while Rob loaded the dishwasher.

Rob stopped what he was doing and pulled up the Notes app on his phone. "Sam and Jon land a few minutes past eleven this morning. Kyle's flight gets in a little before noon, and Julie arrives at one-fifteen. They're all in United business class, so Sam, Jon, and Kyle will wait in the Star Alliance Arrivals Lounge until Julie shows up."

"Okay." Ben nodded, taking mental notes.

Rob paused to refill both their cups. "Sam reserved an SUV for the four of them, but I'm sure she's gonna ask Kyle to drive.

And I'm guessing they'll want to stop for lunch on the way here."

"Perfect. I just texted Kyle about the batteries, so he'll see it when he lands. They'll be here in plenty of time for dinner. What do you think we should have?"

"I saw some chicken breasts in the freezer. We could thaw those out, marinate them, and grill them for dinner. I'll make a Greek salad, and there's a loaf of artisan bread; that and a few bottles of white wine should do it."

"Sounds great," Ben said. "Do you feel like going out for a bit? The weather forecast said we may get a small snow flurry later this afternoon or tonight but no real accumulation. It looks nice out now, though; a little exercise might be a good idea."

"Yes, please. We've probably eaten a bit more than usual on this trip; let's see if we can burn some of it off."

"I can think of a few ways we could burn it off by staying in." Ben smiled deviously. He wrapped Rob in a hug and kissed him deeply. "We're only gonna be alone for a few more hours."

Rob kissed him back, then gently pushed him away. "I'm sure you can, you sexy man, but I'm also sure we'll figure out a way to have some sexy times even with everyone else around. Now put your shoes on and grab your coat. We're going for a walk."

"Yes, boss." Ben snickered as he left to get his shoes.

A COUPLE OF HOURS LATER, they were back from their stroll and had decided on grilled salmon for lunch. Ben was out on the small patio outside of the kitchen, trying to light the built-in gas grill. After a few tries, he finally got it lit and returned to the kitchen.

"The grill will be ready in a few minutes."

Rob had prepared a miso glaze for the fish and made a salad as a side dish. "Great. Once the grill is ready, it won't take long to cook the salmon."

Ben's phone buzzed; he dug it out of his pocket to read the screen.

"Kyle just got to the arrivals lounge and is with Sam and Jon. He got my text and is happy to stop at Tesco's on their way here. He wants to know if we need anything else."

"I can't think of anything," Rob said.

Ben texted Kyle back to let him know they were all set, then took the platter with the glazed fish and headed out the door.

Rob gathered plates and flatware and set them on the island. The cobalt-and-yellow-striped placemats were still there from breakfast, and he retrieved bright canary yellow napkins from a drawer before filling two tall glasses with ice and sparkling water. He found some limes in the fridge and cut a couple of wedges to add to their beverages. A few minutes later, Ben returned with the perfectly grilled fish, and they chatted about the coming week while they ate.

LATER THAT AFTERNOON, they sat in the family room. Ben read on his Kindle, and Rob worked on a few logo ideas for a friend who was starting up a new consulting business. He was studying the screen of his MacBook intently when he heard a car pull up. Ditching their devices, they both headed to the foyer.

Ben opened the front door just as Kyle was reaching for the knob.

"Hey guys," Ben said, hugging Kyle and kissing his cheek. The four new arrivals made their way into the foyer, and Sam took the opportunity to introduce her cousin.

"Jon, this is Ben and Rob," she said, pointing out the men. "Rob, Ben, this is my cousin, Jon Rivera."

"Thank you so much for letting me barge in on your family celebration," Jon said. "I really appreciate it."

His voice was deep, but he was soft-spoken, and his dark brown eyes reflected the sincerity in his words. He was a large man—easily six-feet-four with broad shoulders and a trim waist. Clearly, he worked out regularly. His black hair was short and spiky with a bit of gray at the temples, matching the light flecks in his short, neatly trimmed beard.

"We're very glad that Sam asked you to come along. She's family to us, so that automatically means that you're family too," Rob said. They shook hands warmly, then hugs continued with Sam, Julie, and Kyle.

"Let's get your luggage, and we'll show you your rooms, so you can take a few minutes to get settled," Ben told them. "Then we can relax for a bit before dinner."

After bringing everyone upstairs and showing the group around, Ben and Rob resumed their seats in the sitting room. A few minutes later, Julie walked in.

"Your home is beautiful, Ben!" she exclaimed. "I can't believe I never visited before."

"Thanks, Julie. And it's not like you haven't been invited." Ben smiled.

"If I'd known, I definitely would have been here sooner."

Julie was a petite woman with very short brown hair and flawless latte skin. Her deep chocolate eyes danced behind bright orange-colored glasses that matched her sweater. Earlier, Ben had told Rob that Julie was forty, but Rob thought she easily looked ten years younger.

"How was the flight?" Rob asked.

"Good. I managed to sleep a good part of the way. My family kept me busy while I was visiting them in Florida, so I was pretty beat by the time I got to the airport," she said, laughing.

Sam stepped into the family room, quickly followed by Kyle and Jon.

"Oh my God, this place is gorgeous, Ben. I may have to invite myself back again soon," Sam said with mischief in her eyes.

"You know you're welcome anytime, Sam."

Sam and Jon sat on one of the sofas near the fireplace while Ben and Julie sat on the one across the room. Kyle was perched on an arm of the couch, and Rob was seated in a comfortable chair near Sam.

"We're glad you're all finally here," Ben began. "I know I speak for Rob when I say we're really happy that you all decided to spend Christmas with us."

They continued to chat a bit about their flights and things back home.

"Why don't I grab some drinks?" Rob asked. He got up and snatched the ice bucket from the bar, then headed into the kitchen while Ben took drink orders.

Once everyone had their beverages in hand, Sam said, "We

drove by Stonehenge on the way here. I'd love to visit if we have time."

"That shouldn't be a problem," Ben answered. "Mike and Ellen are arriving tomorrow, so I thought we'd stay around here and perhaps go to the pub for dinner, but maybe Tuesday afternoon would work."

"Yeah, I'd like to see it," Julie agreed.

"I've been a few times, but I wouldn't mind going again," Kyle piped up. "What about you, Jon? Are you interested in seeing Stonehenge?"

"Definitely," Jon answered. "I still can't believe I'm here. When Sam said we were coming to England for Christmas, I thought she was joking. I'm pretty much up for anything, and I want to thank you again for your hospitality."

"Like I said before, Jon, you're family, so like it or not you're stuck with us." Rob chuckled. "Right, Sam?"

"Oh, for sure. There's no getting away from you. Not that I'd want to at this point, though. The family you choose, or that chooses you, is often the best family." She reached out and took Rob's hand.

"Amen to that," Kyle said, grinning broadly. He raised his glass, and the others followed suit.

"We figured you'd all be pretty beat from traveling, so we'll just have a quiet evening at home tonight," Rob told the others. "There's chicken marinating in the fridge. We'll grill that whenever you guys are ready to eat. We've also got some crusty bread and a Greek salad to go with it."

"That sounds amazing," Julie chimed in. "And frankly, I could eat."

"Me too," Jon uttered.

"Yeah, I think it's dinner time," Kyle added. "Dad, I can help man the grill if you'd like."

"Okay, people, let's move to the kitchen. I'll grab the wine, and we'll make this happen."

Ben stood and retrieved a few bottles of wine from the bar fridge. The rest of them followed Rob into the kitchen where they all pitched in to get dinner on the table in record time.

CHAPTER 8

Ben was pouring his second cup of coffee when Kyle entered the kitchen.

"Morning, Dad."

"G'morning, son. Coffee?"

"Yes, please."

Ben reached for another mug in the cabinet above the coffee maker and filled it for Kyle. "How'd you sleep?"

"Really well. But I never have problems sleeping here. I don't know if it's the quiet or what, but I always feel more relaxed when I'm here." Kyle sighed, obviously content.

"I know what you mean. I was just telling Rob the other day that I feel the same way whenever I'm here," Ben agreed.

"I had dinner with Uncle Mike and Aunt Ellen a couple of weeks ago, and we talked about this trip," Kyle said. "I have to agree with you, Dad, Uncle Mike definitely didn't seem all that excited about coming here, but I'm not sure why."

"Hmmm, so it's not just me," Ben replied. "I spoke to him the week after Thanksgiving, and he just didn't seem into it at all. Did he say anything specific when you saw him?"

"No, that's just it; he never said he didn't want to be together for the holidays. In fact, he seemed really excited about seeing everyone and spending time together. But I got the impression he'd rather do it in DC or something." Kyle knit his eyebrows together. "And now that I think about it, he hasn't come out here for several years now. Maybe it's something about this place?"

"I suppose that's possible, but I never got that feeling from him before. From what I remember, we both have lots of good memories of this place. I'm gonna try and talk to him about it. Maybe tomorrow. I don't want him to be unhappy, but I'd also really like to know what's going on."

Rob walked into the kitchen and made a beeline for the coffee maker.

"Morning, guys. Are you talking about Mike?"

"Yeah. Kyle was just saying that he had dinner with him and Ellen a couple of weeks ago, and he got the same feeling —that Mike didn't really want to come here."

"The weird thing is," Kyle added, "Aunt Ellen didn't really say much, and she rarely keeps her opinion to herself."

"Very true," Ben agreed. "I'll see what I can find out tomorrow. But for now, how about some breakfast?"

Eventually, everyone else made their way downstairs, and they all took turns cooking and serving each other.

After breakfast, Kyle offered to play tour guide, so he, Julie, Sam, and Jon decided to take a walk into the village. Before they left, Ben asked Kyle to speak with Carl and see if he could handle eight of them having dinner at the pub that night. Since it was off-season there, Ben didn't want Carl to be unprepared.

As they were leaving, a delivery truck showed up with a Christmas tree and several arrangements of flowers and holiday greenery. Ben helped the driver place the arrangements in the foyer until they decided where to put things, then showed him where to set up the tree in the family room.

Once the driver left, he went in search of Rob to solicit his help in figuring out where to put the flowers and greens. He found Rob in the kitchen making a big pot of soup for lunch.

"Mmmm, that smells delicious," Ben said as he turned the corner from the hallway into the kitchen.

"Thanks. It's vegetable beef with barley. Can you text Kyle and ask him to pick up a loaf or two of bread at the bakery? We can have it for lunch with the soup and whatever's left can be toasted for breakfast."

"Sure. Then you need to help me decide where to put the flowers that just got delivered."

When Ben finished texting Kyle, Rob said, "Okay, this can simmer for a while. Show me what we've got."

Together they managed to find places for all the arrangements, including a low vase containing some tiny white flowers, evergreen sprigs, and some holly with brilliant crimson berries for the kitchen island. Things were starting to look festive at The Mews.

Rob went upstairs to retrieve his laptop. He set it up to work on the island while Ben used his iPad to answer a few emails and surf the web. Every once in a while, Rob would get up and stir the soup, but otherwise they worked together in silence. Sometime later, they heard noise outside, and when Ben looked up, he saw Kyle and the others through the window in the kitchen door.

As he let them in, Jon handed Rob a bag containing two loaves of fresh bread. Rob looked at the clock and realized it was just past twelve-thirty.

"Thanks, Jon. Lunch is just about ready. If you all want to freshen up and help set the table, we can eat."

They all murmured their approval. "Great," Jon said. "I worked up an appetite with all that walking."

"Oh, Dad, I asked Carl about dinner tonight, and he said no problem. He'll make sure we have plenty to eat."

"I'm sure he will. Thanks for checking with him."

Working like a well-oiled machine, they were soon enjoying a delicious lunch.

SHORTLY AFTER LUNCH WAS OVER, and everything was put away, Ben's phone buzzed. He was in the family room with Rob and Sam, trying to organize the lights and ornaments for the tree. They were hoping to get it decorated that night or the next day.

"Mike and Ellen just got their rental car. They're gonna stop for a quick bite on the way but should be here in about three hours."

"That's great," Rob said. "It'll be nice to see them again."

"Yes. And hopefully I'll get a chance to talk to Mike about why he didn't seem thrilled to come here for Christmas." Ben glanced at his watch. "But before they get here, I think I'll take a little nap."

He stared pointedly at Rob and wiggled his eyebrows. "Care to join me?"

"Hmmm, something tells me you have something other than a nap in mind," Sam chuckled.

"Well, there may be something else going on that leads up to the nap," Ben replied innocently.

"Sure, let's go," Rob said, grabbing Ben's hand. "See you later, Sam."

A FEW HOURS LATER, they were all sitting around the family room, chatting about nothing in particular, when Kyle peered out the window facing the front of the house and said, "I think they're here."

Ben and Rob went to the front door to greet Mike and Ellen as they entered. Mike was a couple of years older than Ben and shared a family resemblance, although Mike was a bit taller and heavier. Not that he was out of shape, he just carried a few more pounds. Ellen was of average height and wore her salt-and-pepper hair in a short pixie style that suited her. Her hazel eyes sparkled as she took in the gathering.

Kyle and Jon offered to get their bags from the car, and soon they were all seated in the family room, catching up on Mike and Ellen's travels. Their flight was uneventful, but neither had managed to sleep very much on the plane, so they were both exhausted.

"Why don't you go up and take a little nap?" Ben suggested. "We're going to the pub tonight for dinner; Carl knows we're all coming. You can rest for a couple of hours before we head over there."

"That sounds like a very good idea to me," Ellen declared. She reached over and took her husband's hand and led him upstairs to their room.

"What time is Carl expecting us tonight?" Rob directed his question to Kyle.

"I told him we'd probably be there between six-thirty and seven. I figured Uncle Mike and Aunt Ellen would want to rest a bit when they got here."

"Good thinking," Ben said, gazing proudly at his son. "Seeing that we have some time, how about I get some drinks for us, and maybe we can play a game. I saw a Mexican Train set behind the bar."

Rob got the box of dominoes and handed it to Kyle. "Can you get this set up on the table, and I'll help your dad get drinks?"

"Sure. C'mon, guys, let's get ready to play."

CHAPTER 9

Monday, December 21 – later that day

Despite the cool temperature, there was no wind, so the group decided to walk to the pub. It only took about ten minutes, and they knew the exercise would do them good.

A fire at the hearth and warm smiles around the room greeted them when they entered. There were a few locals seated at a couple of the tables as well as along the rail. Sarah stepped out from behind the bar.

"Welcome, my friends. So good to see you all."

She led them to a long table in the corner between the front windows and the fireplace. Everyone got seated, and Sarah took their drink orders.

"I'll be back in a jiffy with those."

A blackboard on the wall listed the fare for the evening—

cottage pie, steak and kidney pie, bangers and mash, and Scotch eggs.

Sarah returned bearing a tray of drinks with Carl following close behind. Once they all had their beverages, Sarah said, "In addition to what's on the board, I can put together a ploughman's plate if anyone would like that. It's typically lunch fare, but some folks like it in the evening too. No judgement here. Oh, and the entrées include a salad. There's no rush. Take your time and relax. Call me over when you're ready to order."

Sarah left, but Carl stayed to chat with everyone. He shook hands with Mike and squeezed Ellen's shoulder fondly. "I'm so very happy you're all here together for the holiday."

"Dad said that Billy and his boyfriend will be here for Christmas," Kyle said. "Hopefully I'll see them on Boxing Day."

"That would be grand, Kyle," Carl replied. "I'm sure they'd love to spend some time with you. It's been a few years now, hasn't it?"

"That it has, Carl," Kyle agreed.

"Well, I best get back behind the bar before the missus gives me hell for shirking my duties," Carl joked with a gleam in his eye. "Let me know when you're ready for another round."

The group sipped their drinks and talked about what they might order. After a few minutes, Ben caught Sarah's attention, so they could place their orders.

"Sam, Julie, Jon, and I are thinking of going to Stonehenge tomorrow. Would anyone like to join us?" Kyle said to the group.

"I might. If I'm not still tired," Ellen said, laughing lightly.

"These long flights take me longer to bounce back from the older I get."

"I'll probably just stick around the house," Mike told them. "I went there enough when we lived here."

Ben couldn't detect anything negative in the tone of Mike's voice, but something seemed off, and it grated on him a bit. It seemed clear to him that Mike really wasn't happy to be there, and he swore to himself that he would get to the bottom of the issue. Since Mike was staying home tomorrow, that might be the perfect time.

"I think I'll stick around the house too," Ben said. "What about you, Rob?"

"I don't know yet. I'll decide in the morning."

Just then, Carl and Sarah arrived with salads for everyone. They ordered another round of drinks and tucked in.

Dinner was wonderful. They all ate well, engaging in lively conversation among themselves and with a few locals. Before they knew it, hours had passed, and they had each consumed more than a few drinks. As they prepared to leave, Rob settled up with Carl and bid him a good night.

They walked back to the house, relieved that none of them had to drive home. The crisp air was revitalizing, but they welcomed the warmth of the house when they finally reached it.

Mike and Ellen excused themselves, saying they needed more sleep, and headed off to bed. Julie quickly followed; everyone else decided on a nightcap before retiring.

Tuesday, December 22 – at The Mews

. . .

Ben found Mike and Ellen enjoying some coffee when he entered the kitchen. "Good morning. Did you guys sleep well?"

"I certainly did," Ellen replied. "And I'm pretty sure Mike did as well."

"I did indeed," Mike agreed.

"Excellent," Ben said, pouring himself a much-needed cup of coffee. "Did you decide to go to Stonehenge with the group, Ellen?"

"I think I'm just going to stick close to the house today. I may go out for a bit of exercise and then nap this afternoon."

Rob and Sam ambled into the kitchen, and Rob immediately went for the coffee pot.

"Good morning," he said to everyone, still sounding a bit groggy. He poured the rest of the coffee into cups for himself and Sam and then started a new pot.

Eventually, everyone else wandered down for breakfast and helped themselves to food and coffee. There was yogurt, bread, scones, and fruit salad, so it was easy for everyone to serve themselves.

After breakfast, Ellen, Sam, and Julie decided to go out for a stroll. When they returned, Rob and Kyle were putting lunch together. There was leftover soup heating on the stove and some grilled chicken breasts from a couple of nights earlier that Kyle sliced for sandwiches.

"We can leave for Stonehenge after lunch," said Kyle. "Who's coming?"

Sam, Julie, and Jon raised their hands. It would just be the four of them, as Ellen wanted to take a nap, and Rob planned on doing a bit more work on the logos he was designing. Once the group left for sightseeing, Rob made himself a cup of tea and went to the family room with his laptop to work for a while.

Ben walked down the hall from the foyer and heard noise coming from the office behind the family room. He poked his head in and saw Mike sitting behind their dad's old desk in the corner.

"Hey, Mike. What's going on?"

Mike shrugged. "Not much. Just looking around at stuff and remembering old times."

"Do you have a minute?" Ben asked cautiously. "There's something I wanted to talk to you about."

"Of course, Ben. What's on your mind?"

"Ever since I brought up the idea of coming here for the holidays, I've gotten the feeling that this isn't something you really wanted to do. Did you not want to spend Christmas with us?"

"No, that's not it at all," Mike said. "I was happy to spend time with you guys, but if I'm being honest, I wasn't all that thrilled about coming back to The Mews."

"Why?" Ben was puzzled. "Don't you like it here?"

"Not really," Mike admitted. "I don't have the same fond memories of this place that you have. Don't get me wrong, it was okay when we were here as kids, but things were so cut and dried as I got older. I never told you this, but Dad really wanted me to follow in his footsteps and work for the government. That wasn't really something I was interested in."

Mike paused, and Ben kept silent, sensing that Mike was trying to collect his thoughts. "When I told him and Mom that I wanted to study law, he thought it would be a way into politics and government, but when I explained I was more interested in family law, Dad was clearly disappointed. He tried for a long time to talk me out of it, and a lot of those discussions happened right here in this room. I have to admit, after all these years, it still leaves me feeling unsettled. Part of me hates this place because of those memories."

"Oh, Mike, I had no idea!" Ben was shocked. "Why didn't you ever tell me?"

"Well, I didn't really want to talk about it when it was happening, and later on, it was sort of 'water under the bridge,' ya know? Dad and I got to a point where we just agreed to disagree about it, and Mom did her best not to take sides. I know she understood my feelings about it all but didn't say much. I don't think she wanted to piss off Dad any more than I had already done."

Ben chuckled. "Yeah, that was Mom all right. She never liked conflict. Tried to be neutral and make everyone happy. I guess I need to apologize for making you come here. I never would have pushed if I'd known."

"It's fine, Ben. I'm not upset with you about it. True, I'm not all that thrilled to be here, but I am happy to be with family, and I guess that's the important thing." Mike eyed Ben. "But now that we're talking about this, I have a question for you."

"Okay," Ben replied, unsure of what was coming next.

Mike took a deep breath and seemed hesitant to continue.

Finally, he looked Ben directly in the eyes. "How would you feel about selling this place?"

"Huh? No." Ben was flabbergasted. "Um, that's not really something that I'd consider. I love this place. Oh, wait. Is that really what *you* want to do?"

"Yeah. I'm sorry, but it really is. Ellen and I have been talking; her health scare a few years ago kinda put a new perspective on our lives."

"Ellen's okay, right? The cancer's not back or anything, is it?" Ben felt his eyes grow, and he panicked a bit, worried that Ellen was sick again.

Four years earlier, Ellen had been diagnosed with breast cancer, and they'd all rallied around as a family to support one another. It was a difficult time for them all, but the cancer had been caught early, and after surgery, chemo, and radiation treatments, the doctors were confident that things were under control.

"No, nothing like that. Ellen's fine. She goes for regular checkups but hasn't had any other issues, thank God." Ben breathed a sigh of relief as Mike continued, "But it's made us think about our future a bit differently, and I'm probably gonna retire in the next couple of years. I've made some good investments, but still, selling this place would give me an added infusion of cash to make our retirement just a bit easier. We're hoping to be able to travel a bit more, especially to California to see Mike Jr. and our new grandchild."

Mike paused as if trying to figure out what to say next. "Can you at least think about it? Selling this place, I mean. I really have no desire to ever come back here again. I've done some preliminary inquiries, and I'm told we could get a handsome price for the place."

Ben whistled at the figure Mike threw out. "Wow. I had no idea. How about I promise to think about it and discuss it with Rob. I have to admit that as much as I want to help you out, Mike, it really hurts to think about losing this place."

A strange look crossed Mike's face when Ben mentioned

that he wanted to discuss it with Rob. "Look, Ben, I know you and Rob have gotten close over the past year, but is this really something you want to talk with him about? I just don't want you to get hurt. I'd hate to see him take advantage of you because you're 'rich and famous,' ya know?" Mike said, adding air quotes around "rich and famous."

Ben glared at him. "What the fuck, Mike? It's not like that at all. Where the hell is this coming from? Rob is not with me because he's after my money!"

Mike didn't look the least bit apologetic, and that made Ben even more enraged. "Are you really sure, Ben? Again, I don't want you to get hurt by anyone."

"As much as I appreciate your concern, Mike, I just have to say fuck you. I can't tell you how hurt and angry this makes me. You have no fucking idea …" He trailed off, unable to continue speaking.

"It wouldn't be the first time someone tried to take advantage of someone's wealth and popularity, Ben. I just want what's best for you."

Ben was practically shouting now. "He's what's best for me, Mike. And for your information—even though it's really none of your business—he probably has more money than you and I put together." He turned on his heel and stormed out of the office. Mike stared after him, his mouth agape.

"What do you mean? Ben? Ben, wait!"

Ben grabbed his coat from the foyer closet and rushed out the front door, slamming it harder than he intended.

Rob flew out of the family room and stared at Mike. "What happened?"

"I said something that upset him," Mike said, his face reddening. "He ran out of the house."

Rob raced after Ben, pulling on his coat. He saw Ben walking along the path past the carriage house; it led along the woods behind the property.

When he finally caught up with him and touched his arm, Ben turned, ready to lash out at Mike again, before realizing it was Rob who'd followed him out of the house.

"What's wrong, sweetheart?" Rob said gently, concern wrapped around his words. "Talk to me."

"My brother," Ben started, his face scarlet, "is an arrogant fucking son of a bitch!"

Rob reared back, looking aghast at Ben. "Okay. Now before you tell me what happened, take a deep breath and try to calm down. Having a heart attack right now isn't going to help the situation."

They slowed down a bit while Ben took a few deep breaths. They were passing a partial stone wall near the woods, and Ben stopped to rest against it.

"I found Mike in the office and asked him about why he wasn't thrilled about coming here for Christmas."

"Fine. What did he say?"

Ben relayed the rest of the story, trying his best to not get worked up all over again. When he revealed what the estate was possibly worth, Rob whistled as Ben had. "Wow, that's impressive."

Ben finished the story, adding that Mike was an overprotective prick who'd made the worst assumptions about Rob's intentions. The anger bubbled forth again, and from the look on Ben's face, he was fighting hard to keep it in check. "How dare he assume the worst? What a fucking asshole!"

"Calm down, baby. It's not his fault he didn't know about me having a lot of money. We never told him because we didn't think it mattered, so that's on us. But really, he was only looking out for you."

Rob reached over and put his arm around Ben, rubbing slow circles across his shoulders.

"He doesn't want you to get hurt, and he had no way of knowing that the money wasn't what drew me to you. You and I both know it was your big cock and those wicked things you do with your mouth." Rob snickered, an evil glint in his eyes.

Ben laughed, grateful for Rob's lighthearted humor. "I love you so much. Thank you for talking me off the ledge *and* making me laugh in the process."

"Hey, we take care of each other. Remember, we're a team." Rob paused, a faraway look shadowing his eyes. Ben could tell he was sorting something out in his head, so he stayed quiet and concentrated on his breathing and staying calm.

Suddenly, Rob turned to Ben with a gleam in his eye and smiled. "Okay, I think I may have a solution that will make everyone happy."

"Really? Tell me."

"Well, I just sold my condo in Florida, and you're talking about selling your place in LA and moving in with me, right?" Rob carried on, not waiting for Ben to answer. "Plus, I do have a sizable chunk of cash socked away in several different investments, thanks to Alan's foresight. I could liquidate something, and if we combine the condo money, your house money, and one or two of my investments, we could buy Mike out. I'd still have enough left in the other investments to keep my regular income."

Ben's eyes widened, and his mouth hung open, amazed that Rob would make such an offer. "No, Rob. I can't ask you to do that," Ben protested, shock and amazement still showing on his face.

"You didn't. I offered. Because I love you and want you to be happy. Besides, I know I've only been here a few days, but I love this place, and it would really make me happy to be able to keep it in the family."

Ben turned to him, kissing him tenderly.

"You'd really do that?"

"Of course. I just said we're a team, right? We're in this together." Rob smiled.

"I love you so much. How'd I get so lucky?"

"I love you too," Rob told him. "You realize that we both got lucky, right? But now you need to go back and apologize to

Mike. He was only looking out for his baby brother. Then tell him you have a solution."

"Okay. Let's do this." Ben grabbed Rob's hand and they hurried back to the house.

BEN AND ROB entered the house and Ben saw Mike in the family room sipping an amber liquid from a crystal rocks glass. He guessed it was bourbon, Mike's alcoholic beverage of choice. Mike glanced up as Ben walked into the room. By the look on his face, Ben knew that he was upset.

"Mike, I want to apologize for how I reacted," Ben blurted out before Mike had a chance to say anything. "I realize now that you were only looking out for me. I'm sorry I yelled and ran out."

"I'm the one who should apologize, Ben. I should have handled that differently. You were right to be angry with me," Mike confessed.

Rob waited in the foyer for a moment, then started toward the hall, leaving Ben and his brother to talk about what had happened.

"Rob, wait," Mike called out. "I'd like to speak with you if I may."

Rob pivoted toward the family room, and Ben could see the uncertainty in his body language.

"I'm sorry I questioned your feelings toward my brother," Mike said. "I should have spoken to both of you about this earlier. It wasn't my intention to doubt you, really. I just wanted to protect my brother."

"I understand what you were trying to do, Mike. But what

you said to Ben hurt me, and you hurt Ben even more by not trusting him. I'm sure we can move past all of this, but we're all going to have to work together and communicate better."

"I appreciate it." Mike reached for Ben and Rob at the same time, and they group-hugged.

"How about we have a drink, and Ben can tell me how much of an ass I've been?" Mike joked.

"Permission to call you an ass again? Works for me." Ben chuckled.

Mike went around the bar and pulled out two more glasses and poured them each a healthy measure of bourbon.

As they raised their glasses, Ben said, "To my brother, the ass."

They drank, then sat near the fireplace. Ben looked pointedly at his brother and said, "You really did hurt me, Mike, but Rob made me realize that you had the best intentions, so I forgive you. Just don't be an ass again. You can always talk to me, but I'm a grown man, and I can make my own decisions. You don't have to protect me all the time, you know."

"Yeah, I get it, Ben," Mike agreed. "I didn't mean to come on so strong and take over. You know I can get bullheaded. I just want you safe and happy."

"I'm both safe and happy. Believe that."

Ben paused, waiting to see if Mike had any reaction to that. Mike remained silent but looked chagrined, so Ben continued, "For what it's worth, I think we've come up with a solution to the house situation."

"Really? When did you have time to do that?"

"When I stormed out, and Rob came to find me. It's actually his idea."

"I'm even more intrigued now." Mike turned his attention to Rob. "What's your solution, Rob?"

"I suggested to Ben that we buy your share of the house."

"Wha—" Mike started to interrupt, but Rob pushed forward.

"He's been talking about selling his home in LA, and I just sold my condo in Florida. I have several different investments that I'm not using for income right now, and I can liquidate a couple of those. That would give us the money to buy you out and not really leave me in any financial straits. It gives you what you want and keeps The Mews in the family."

Mike appeared dumbfounded. "You'd do that?"

"Of course I would, Mike. I love your brother." Rob took that moment to look directly into Mike's eyes. "*And* his brother, even if he acts like a jerk sometimes." He smiled to let Mike know that he wasn't upset. "You were only doing it out of love, so I get it, even if you went about it in the wrong way. I want you all to be happy, and if I can help make that happen, I'm more than willing."

"I don't know what to say," Mike admitted. "Thank you. And apologies again for not trusting in you. Until Ben said something earlier, I had no idea you were that financially secure."

"It's fine, Mike. We don't really talk about it much. The truth is, my late husband Alan and I hit the lottery several years ago, and Alan invested most of the money very wisely. It was one of those multi-state lotteries, and we won several million dollars. Ben has known from the beginning that I was well-off, so he knew I wasn't going after him for his wealth or fame. We probably should have told you and Ellen about it, but we really didn't think it was an issue."

Ben blushed, remembering what Rob had said earlier about loving him for his big cock, but he wisely remained silent.

"I'm totally to blame," Mike said. "I made assumptions without knowing all the facts. That's all on me. Thanks for being so gracious about it. But wait. Ben, if you're planning on selling the LA house, where are you gonna live?"

"I talked to Rob about living with him in Westport. Hell, this past year I spent more time there than I did in LA anyway, so that house is kind of a waste."

"Well then, congratulations. I'm really happy for both of you."

"Thanks," Ben and Rob said simultaneously.

"Mike," Rob interjected. "As far as I'm concerned we're family, so as long as we discuss things like this, we should be okay. I believe we'll all be better off if we stop making assumptions and just talk more. Okay?" Glancing at his watch, Rob continued, "I'm gonna see what I can organize in the way of snacks. The gang will be back from Stonehenge soon, and I'm sure they'll be wanting something to nibble on before dinner. I found a huge tray of lasagna in the freezer and pulled that out to thaw earlier, so dinner is under control. And we have a tree to decorate tonight."

"I'll join you in a few minutes, sweetheart," Ben said, proud of his man.

After Rob left, Mike turned to Ben. "He's really something special. I'm sorry I doubted you, Ben. I can't tell you how happy I am that you found him."

"Thanks, Mike. I'm a very lucky man."

"That you are, brother."

CHAPTER 11

After they'd all indulged in a wonderful dinner of Mrs. Harrison's lasagna, the group moved to the family room to decorate the Christmas tree.

"Rob and I went to the carriage house a few days ago and pulled out all the decorations," Ben announced. "We should probably start with the lights, right?"

"If someone can get drinks for those who might want them, yes, the rest of us can start with the lights," Sam joked.

"I'm at your service, Sam," Ben told her. "What would you like?"

After gathering drink orders, Ben and Rob went about mixing them and opening the wine.

Kyle had found a small stepstool in the entrance hall closet and climbed up on it while Mike handed strings of lights to him. Once the lights were arranged, they opened boxes of decorations and began to trim the tree.

"Oh, hang on!" Rob said suddenly. "I bought an ornament at Harrod's specifically to commemorate our first Christmas in England. Let me go get it."

He ran up to his and Ben's room while the rest of the gang continued to decorate the tree.

A few minutes later, Rob returned and found the perfect spot front and center for the Harrods ornament.

Once the decorations were all in place they added tinsel, giving the tree a silvery, glistening shimmer. The tasks went quickly since there were so many of them working together.

Once they were all satisfied that the tree was fully trimmed, Mike took the star out of one of the boxes and handed it to Kyle.

"Kyle, as the youngest of the family gathered here, you get to place the star at the top."

Kyle used the stepstool again and placed the golden metallic star on the top of the tree. It felt like Christmas was finally there when they all stood back and admired their work.

"It's beautiful," Julie exclaimed.

"I think we did a fine job," Jon added.

Well done, everyone," Ellen said.

They refreshed their drinks and sat around, chatting and appreciating each other's company in the magnificent glow of the Christmas tree.

BEN WAS STANDING at the sink when Rob entered the bathroom. He stared at Ben's ass, clad only in black boxer briefs, then grabbed his toothbrush, hip-checked his lover, and smiled. Ben spit, then wiped his mouth and kissed Rob lightly on the cheek.

"Don't be long, sweetheart."

"I won't," Rob mumbled around his toothbrush.

A few minutes later, he turned off the bathroom light and gasped as he walked toward the bed.

Ben was lying naked in the middle of the king-sized bed, slowly stroking his thickening cock.

"See something you like?"

Rob quickly lowered his boxers and climbed in between Ben's legs. He swatted Ben's hand away from his dick, then slowly licked from root to tip. Kissing the head of Ben's cock, he moved up his body and plunged his tongue into Ben's mouth.

They kissed deeply as Rob felt his ass being spread open. Ben's finger teased his hole, and Rob moaned into the kiss. Rubbing their hardness against each other, they continued to kiss slowly, Rob savoring Ben's taste.

"Love you. So much." Rob panted, flipping them over so that Ben was above him. "I want you inside me. Please," he begged.

"Gladly, my love." Ben reached for the bottle of lube from the nightstand. Slicking his fingers, he teased Rob's pucker again, breaching him with a finger and stretching him.

"More. I need more," Rob pleaded.

Ben added a second finger, then a third, quickening his pace.

"I'm ready. Fuck me now," Rob demanded. "Don't make me wait any longer."

Ben poured more lube on his fingers and coated his rigid

cock. Lining up the head against Rob's hole, he pushed forward, passing the tight ring of muscles. He moved slowly but steadily, stopping once he was fully seated, and his balls rested against Rob.

"So good," he moaned, bending to take Rob's mouth in a searing kiss.

Breaking the kiss, Rob said firmly, "Move, dammit. I want it hard and fast tonight."

"Anything you need." Ben began slowly but sped up as Rob's hands moved from his ass up to his back and hugged him tightly.

Ben switched his position slightly, and they found their rhythm as the head of Ben's dick hit Rob's sensitive bundle of nerves. Rob saw stars.

"That's it. Yes. Again!" Rob almost screamed but forced himself to keep it close to a whisper as best he could. He really didn't want to wake the rest of the house and alert everyone to their activities.

Rob reached for his cock but Ben grabbed it first and stroked him in time with his movements. After a few moments, Rob's balls tightened up against his body, and he knew he was close. Ben continued moving in and out of Rob's ass and quickened the pace of his strokes on Rob's dick.

"Coming!" Rob panted as he pulled Ben down into a scorching kiss, and he orgasmed on both of their stomachs. Rob's ass clenching as he came was all Ben needed, and he quickly spilled into Rob's body.

His movements slowed, but when he started to pull out, Rob's hand on his ass stopped him.

"Stay there for a moment, please. I love feeling you inside of me."

Ben captured Rob's mouth in yet another kiss, this time slow and gentle. Their breathing quieted, and they nipped at each other's mouths, smiling.

Rob loved this feeling after they made love: the closeness, the feeling of being with the most important person in the world.

"I love you," he whispered, not wanting to break the mood.

"Love you back," Ben said quietly. He slipped out of Rob and went to the bathroom to get a wet towel. After cleaning up, they slipped beneath the covers, reaching for each other.

Kissing Rob sweetly, Ben turned over so that he was the little spoon, and Rob wrapped his arms around Ben, pulling him close.

"Good night, love."

CHAPTER 12

Ben and Rob woke still wrapped in each other's arms, just lying there enjoying the warmth of their bodies pressed together.

"I smell coffee," Ben eventually said. "We should probably get up."

Rob sighed sleepily. "You're right. I was gonna ask Sam if she felt like going for a walk this morning. We haven't spent much time together on this trip, and I'd like to fix that."

"Okay. I'll take responsibility for getting lunch together. I know there's a little bit of soup left if anyone wants it, and I can cook some chicken for chicken salad. Can you stop by the bakery on your walk and get a couple loaves of bread for sandwiches?"

"Absolutely. Let's shower and then get some coffee."

When they arrived in the kitchen twenty minutes later, they found Sam, Julie, and Jon enjoying yogurt, toast, and coffee.

"I just put another pot on. It should be ready soon," Sam said, gesturing to the coffee pot. "I'm guessing you both need some caffeine."

"Thanks." Rob picked up Sam's cup and took a sip. They both drank their coffee black, so Rob knew there were no surprises like cream or sugar to spoil that first sip.

"Hey," Sam protested, but she smiled, so Rob knew she wasn't upset.

"I'll refill your cup once the pot's done."

Ben sliced some bread that was on the counter and placed it in the toaster oven for Rob and himself. He pulled two cups from the cupboard and waited by the coffee pot, tapping his foot impatiently.

"Sam, I'm going to take a walk into town this morning to grab some bread for the lunch that Ben's making for us. Come with me? We haven't had much time to chat on this trip; I figured we could catch up."

Sam smiled warmly at Rob. "That sounds good. It looks like it's gonna snow, but the weather forecast said it wouldn't start until later this afternoon. And you're right about not chatting very much. We talk more at home when we're not living under the same roof."

Rob chuckled. "You're so right, Sam." He loved Sam like a sister and was extremely grateful for their friendship. He couldn't imagine life without Sam.

Ben poured coffee for himself and Rob and topped off Sam's cup while Rob buttered their toast. "Snow's not all that unusual here, but we rarely get more than a dusting, so I wouldn't worry about it."

"G'morning, everyone." Kyle entered the kitchen and headed straight for the coffee pot, squeezing Jon's shoulder as he passed him. "How's everyone feeling today?"

Sam glanced knowingly at Rob, but he didn't get what she was trying to say.

They all murmured their replies, "Fine."

"Good."

"Slept really well."

"I heard some strange noises coming from your room last night, Dad. Was everything okay?" Kyle smirked.

"Um, oh, yeah. Everything was fine," Ben stammered.

Rob felt heat trickle into his cheeks and turned away quickly.

Sam and Julie giggled, and Jon outright laughed.

"Kyle, can you take a package of chicken breasts out of the freezer and put it in a bowl of cold water in the sink, please?" Ben asked quickly, hoping to change the subject. "I'm gonna make some chicken salad for lunch."

"Sure, Pops."

Patting his dad on the back, Kyle smirked and stage-whispered "Way to go."

Rob saw Ben smile back at him while fighting to look stern. "Behave yourself."

Sam unsuccessfully covered another giggle with a cough.

"What's going on?" Mike asked as he and Ellen entered the kitchen.

"Oh, nothing really," Kyle said innocently. "I just heard some weird noises from Dad's room last night, and I wanted to make sure everything was okay."

"Weird noises?" Mike repeated.

Rob cleared his throat, feeling the heat once again creep into his face. At the same time, Ben shook his head and closed his eyes.

"Oh, um, right," Mike stammered, his face revealing that he finally understood what Kyle was hinting at.

Ellen just smiled and shook her head.

"Okay, people, nothing to see here. Move along." Ben was still trying to look serious, but Rob could see a twinkle in his eye.

Julie and Jon rinsed cups and plates and loaded the dishwasher while Kyle made a fresh pot of coffee for Mike and Ellen.

"I'm going to brush my teeth and grab my wallet. I'll meet you at the front door in a few minutes, okay, Sam?"

"Sure, that works."

Jon and Mike stayed in the kitchen, quietly talking as they sipped their coffee. Earlier in the week, Jon had mentioned that he was a paralegal at a family law office in Phoenix and was excited to learn that Mike was a lawyer in DC. As Rob and Sam left the kitchen to head upstairs, they heard Jon asking Mike all sorts of questions about the office where he worked.

THE AIR WAS crisp and the sky a dull gray when Rob and Sam left on their stroll to town. They'd bundled up for the weather, though, and felt fine as long as they kept moving.

"So we found out what was bugging Mike about coming to England for Christmas," Rob revealed.

"Oh yeah?" Sam replied. "What's the problem?"

"It seems Mike's not really all that fond of the place. Doesn't have the same kind of memories that Ben has from growing up here. It appears that his dad was pressuring him to follow in his footsteps and go into government work, and that's not what Mike wanted to do. I guess a lot of those conversations happened in his dad's office here in the house. Add to that the fact that he wants to retire in the next year or so to the mix, and he told Ben that he wants to sell the place."

"Oh no. I know how much Ben loves The Mews. How did that go over?"

"Not well. Mike was also afraid that I was interested in Ben only for his money, and Mike warned Ben not to get too attached to me." Rob watched Sam closely, anticipating her reaction to that revelation.

"What? That fucker! I'll kill him!" Sam roared. "No one talks shit about you two."

"Calm down, Sam. It's okay. We got it all worked out."

"What happened?" she asked, obviously trying to slow her breathing and calm down.

"Well, Ben basically told Mike that he was an ass, and that he didn't know what he was talking about. He said that I probably had more money than the two of them put together. But he was so pissed he stormed out of the house, and I had to run after him."

"That sucks. But at least you were there. I'm sure you were able to talk him down, right?"

"Yeah. I made him understand that even though Mike handled it incorrectly, he was only looking out for his little brother. It's partly our fault as well. We never talked about the money stuff with Mike and Ellen, 'cause we didn't think it was all that important. Kyle knew a little about it, but I guess he didn't feel it was his place to say anything to Mike, and Mike evidently didn't ask him."

"Ugh. Why do people get all twisted up about money?"

"I don't know," Rob admitted. "But then I had an idea that I thought would solve everything."

"Oh really, what did ..." Sam started. Suddenly her eyes widened, and she smiled. "Oh, wait! I know what that means. You offered to buy Mike's portion of the house, didn't you?"

"Exactly," Rob confirmed. He never ceased to be amazed at how well Sam understood him. It was Sam who had kicked his butt a year earlier when he was alone and miserable, still mourning the death of Alan. She convinced him that flying to Barcelona and getting on a cruise ship all by himself was exactly what he needed, and of course she was right. Thanks to her, he ended up meeting Ben and falling in love.

"Well," Rob continued, "It makes the most sense. I just sold the place in Florida, and Ben's been talking about selling his house in LA and making Westport his home base. Plus ..." Rob trailed off for effect.

"Wait ... what?" Sam exclaimed. "Ben's gonna move in with you permanently? Woo-hoo!"

"I take it you approve?" Rob chuckled.

"Hell, yes. About fuckin' time, don't ya think? He's so obviously crazy about you. And I know you feel the same about him."

"Yes, I'm really happy about it too. It does feel like it's the right time." Rob paused dreamily, then finished telling Sam about the plan he and Ben had come up with.

"That's a great solution," Sam said, clearly happy with how things were progressing. "That way Mike gets the money he wants for retirement, and Ben gets to keep the house. Well,

I guess the two of you get to keep the house. Did you guys talk to Mike about it?"

"Yeah. Once Ben cooled down, we went back to the house, and they apologized to each other," Rob said. "Mike also admitted that he had unfairly judged me and said he was sorry. We all forgave each other and had a drink together."

"Oh, good," Sam replied, relief in her voice. "I didn't notice any tension in the air when we got back from Stonehenge yesterday, so I think everybody's feeling okay now."

"Yeah, they can both be quite stubborn, but once they realized what was going on, they were able to see things more clearly." Rob chuckled. "From the way all of this unfolded, I'm guessing their dad was stubborn as well, and that's where they get it from, but as long as they talk more and don't go assuming anything, I think it will all be okay."

"I'm sure it will be," Sam replied.

"There's something else I wanted to talk to you about," Rob said, changing the subject. "Why are Ben and I booked on two one-way flights for this trip?"

"Um, well, there was a sale going on, and it was cheaper to book separate flights than a round trip," Sam stuttered, pointedly *not* looking at Rob.

"Nice try, Sam. I know when you're lying to me." Rob grinned. "What's really going on?"

"Okay. See, there was this, um ..." Sam trailed off. "Oh hell. Can you just trust me and leave this alone for now? Please? I can't get into it at the moment, but it's gonna be fine. Really. And you'll know everything soon."

This time, Sam stared intently at Rob, and he knew she was being quite serious.

"Okay, sure. I'm sorry I pushed. It just didn't seem right, and I was curious."

"I knew you'd be suspicious, but please be patient just a little while longer. There's nothing wrong, and it's gonna be amazing." Sam practically glowed. "Ben asked me ..." Sam looked panic-stricken. "Shit."

Rob's eyes bulged, and he smiled at her. "Hmmm, so Ben's behind all of this. I knew it. Tell me."

"No. Leave me alone. I'm not saying another word."

Sam moved away in a huff, but Rob could tell she wasn't upset, she just didn't want to get tricked into saying anything more.

"Okay. I promise I won't badger you anymore. If you say it's okay, I believe you. I won't ask you anything else."

"It's fine, Rob. Do you know how difficult it is to surprise you? But I guess you're worth it." Sam laughed, hip-checking him as they continued into town.

ROB SAUNTERED INTO THE KITCHEN, kissed Ben on the cheek, and handed him two loaves of multigrain bread.

"Thanks, sweetie," Ben said, stealing an extra kiss.

"I'm gonna drop my shoes and wallet upstairs, and then I'll be back to help you get everything ready for lunch, okay?"

"Take your time. I think everything's under control," Ben assured him. "Kyle helped me with the chicken salad, and it's chilling in the fridge now. I'll start heating the soup in a little while."

"Cool. See you in a few."

Rob went quickly up the stairs and into Sam's room. She handed him two boxes as soon as he entered.

Opening the top box, Rob gasped. "Oh my God, it's gorgeous!"

The bracelet consisted of a half circle of platinum joined with a length of dark brown leather to form the other half of the bracelet. The leather ended in a loop with a platinum adjustable bead around a simple round clasp shaped like a compass rose, and there was a diamond in the center of this one. Opening the second box revealed its mate, identical except for the ruby instead of a diamond.

"I can't wait to give this to him. Thanks for bringing them to me, Sam."

"Of course, sweetie. He's gonna love it."

"Let me hide these while he's downstairs. I'll see you in a few."

He gave her a quick hug and kiss and set out to find a good hiding place in their bedroom.

CHAPTER 13

Thursday, December 24 – Christmas Eve

Like every other morning, the group slowly convened in the kitchen for coffee and a bite to eat. They were more aware of the time this morning and hurried to clean up after themselves, as Mrs. Harrison and the women from town would be arriving before lunch to prep the food for their Christmas celebration.

The ladies arrived at ten-thirty, and after introductions and hugs—as Mrs. Harrison hadn't seen Kyle, Mike, or Ellen in a while—Ben offered to make coffee or tea for them.

"Nonsense," Mrs. Harrison said. "We'll take care of that, dear. You go off and relax. This is your holiday. We're just getting a few things ready, chopping vegetables and such. It shouldn't take us more than a couple of hours. I'll be back tomorrow to finish it all up and get it on the table."

Knowing it was best not to argue with Mrs. H, the group made themselves scarce after securing a promise that she'd find Ben or Rob before they all left for the day.

Ben and Julie spent time in the office going over his calendar and some upcoming meetings, while Rob and Sam sat in the family room chatting about friends back home. Kyle and Jon decided to go for a walk. It had snowed a bit the night before, just a light dusting, although more was expected later in the day.

"There's something I wanted to ask you," Sam said to Rob, keeping her voice low. "Yesterday at breakfast, did you happen to notice what Kyle did when he walked into the kitchen?"

"Um, not really. He got coffee, right?"

"Yeah, but as he walked in, he squeezed Jon's shoulder. It seemed a bit, I dunno, intimate. You don't think there's anything going on between them, do you?"

"Shit, really?" Rob's eyes bulged, but a hint of a smile appeared on his face. "I have no idea. It's not like Kyle has ever really talked about his sexuality with Ben. I mean, Ben thinks he may be gay or bi, but it's not an issue, so Ben hasn't pressed him for any details. Do *you* think something's going on?"

"I don't know. I'm not sure I want to ask Jon, either. I mean, he's an adult." Sam shrugged. "So's Kyle, and it's really none of my business."

"I agree, and while I think Jon's a great guy, something tells me Ben might not be too happy with the age difference."

"Fuck, you're right." Sam paused. "What about you? Does it bother you?"

"Not really. If Kyle were eighteen or something, I think I would have a problem with it, but he's twenty-eight, and Jon's what, forty-one? Yeah, that's thirteen years, but as you said, they're both adults," Rob said. "Frankly, if something is going on, I'm kind of happy to think that Kyle may have found someone. But if Jon mentions anything to you, please let me know. I'll do what I can to help Ben deal with the age difference if it becomes an issue."

"Don't worry, I will," Sam agreed, nodding her head.

"And it's probably none of my business, but you never told me what's going on between Jon and his mom. Can you share?"

"Sure, but I think I'd like some wine to go with this conversation. Talking about my aunt always pisses me off." She sounded sad and a bit frustrated.

"Of course. And if you'd rather not talk about it, that's fine. I'll still give you wine." Rob chuckled. "White or red?"

"Red, I think. Thanks. And talking about it is fine, really."

Rob found a bottle of malbec behind the bar and poured them both a generous glassful. Handing Sam the wine, he said, "So what's happening with the Arizona family?"

"I'm pretty sure I told you that my aunt Louisa isn't thrilled that Jon is gay, right?"

Rob nodded, so she continued, "Well, he'd been seeing a guy for a while, and frankly, no one in the family seemed all that fond of this guy. I'm not exactly sure why, as I never met him, but Jon's sister Bernadette described him as a leech. They broke up recently. I'm not sure who did the breaking up part, but I hope it was Jon if the guy was a loser."

"So what's the problem? Yeah, Jon's still gay, but at least he's no longer with this guy."

"This is where it gets really weird. Even though crazy Louisa isn't happy about Jon's sexual preference—ugh, that's her talking, I don't think I've ever heard her actually say the word 'gay'—she was hoping that since he was dating someone, he might finally be settling down. Apparently, she wants more grandkids."

"Wait a minute." Rob was dumbfounded. "She's not happy he's gay but wants him to settle down with a guy who might be a loser, so that he can start a family? She's crazy!"

"Oh, very!" Sam agreed, taking a sip of wine. "And she told him if he couldn't settle down and think about giving her grandchildren before he got too old, she'd disown him— whatever the hell she means by that. Seriously, she's a lunatic. Personally, I think she may need professional help. She's always been a bit narrow-minded, but she's getting worse as she gets older. She's living in his house, but he didn't feel like he could kick her out or anything, so he decided he couldn't stay there right now, and that's how he ended up at my place."

"Unbelievable!" Rob shook his head, dumbfounded. "What's gonna happen now? He's not staying with you long-term, is he?"

"I don't think so. He does have a job that he has to get back to. Fortunately, my aunt lives in an in-law apartment with its own separate entrance, so it's not like he has to see her all that much, but I think it'll still be stressful for him."

"I know you don't wanna hear this, but you're gonna have to talk to him eventually. Granted, he shouldn't have to put up with that shit, but I don't really know what he can do about it, either."

"I know," Sam said, sighing. "He's certainly welcome to stay with me a bit longer if he needs to, but it's not like he can stay away forever. I think I'll call Bernadette when we get home and see if she has any ideas. She's married and has a couple of kids, but their house isn't big enough for Louisa to move in with them. It's too bad, since living in a house with grandkids might really be all she needs to take her mind off Jon."

She paused, then added thoughtfully, "Okay, enough depressing talk about crazy family. Let's talk about something more pleasant."

"Sounds good to me. Actually, I did want to talk to you about a cruise for April or May ..."

ELLEN, Julie, and Sam had offered to prepare Christmas Eve dinner, grilling salmon and serving it with parslied potatoes and green beans. It was a simple and delicious meal, and once everything was cleaned up and put away, they relaxed in the family room listening to holiday music. It was snowing lightly and truly felt like Christmas.

Around ten o'clock, folks started drifting up to bed until just Ben and Rob were left in the family room.

"Thanks so much for suggesting this trip. It's been an amazing time, and I'm sad that it's almost at an end."

"Of course, sweetheart," Ben replied. "It has been wonderful, and it's not quite over yet. I was thinking maybe we could go back to Winchester on Sunday, just the two of us—visit the cathedral, have lunch or dinner somewhere. Maybe even spend the night."

Rob thought it was a great idea. "That sounds wonderful. I've really loved spending time with everyone here, but a little bit of alone time sounds really good."

"Great. I've got a place in mind. I'll give them a call on Saturday morning and see if I can reserve a room. Now, how 'bout we go to bed?"

CHAPTER 14

Friday, December 25 – Christmas Day

Ben awoke to the sound of a truck in the courtyard of the house. The sun was shining brightly through the window, and he could see bits of snow clinging to the mullions. He figured that the snow that had begun in the early evening had continued for a time through the night.

He turned back to Ben and kissed him gently awake. "Merry Christmas, sweetheart."

"Merry Christmas, darling." Rob returned the kiss and hugged him. "I'd love to stay in this warm bed with you, but I suppose we should get up and head downstairs. Besides, I really need to pee."

Rob headed into the bathroom while Ben peered out the window. Sure enough, there were a few inches of snow on the ground, and Mr. Dobbins from town was out there doing a bit of cleanup.

After taking care of business and brushing their teeth, they stumbled down to the kitchen in matching Christmas pajamas—sleep pants featuring dancing reindeer and Christmas trees on a pale blue background with a solid navy T-shirt.

They found Kyle, Jon, and Sam already sitting at the island, enjoying their coffee. They were all in their pajamas as well, but Sam—wearing a red-and-green-plaid sleep outfit—was the only one who came close to a Christmas theme.

Sam poured two more cups when they walked in, and Rob and Ben accepted them gratefully. "Thanks, Sam. Merry Christmas, guys," Rob said sleepily, sipping his much-needed caffeine.

"I'll start another pot, so that it's ready when everyone else comes down," Sam said. Once that task was done, they all went into the family room and gathered near the tree.

Ben picked up a wrapped package and went to the front door. Mr. Dobbins was sweeping the last of the snow from the steps. "Merry Christmas, Mr. Dobbins. Thank you so much for coming by to clean things up."

"No trouble, Master Ben. I know Ethel is coming by later to finish getting your holiday dinner ready, and I didn't want her to have any troubles."

"That's very kind of you, and we really appreciate it." He held out the package. "This is just a little something to help keep you warm on these cold winter nights."

"Much obliged, Master Ben. A Merry Christmas to you and yours. I'll be off now. I've got one more stop to make, then I'm heading to my daughter's for dinner."

Feeling warm with holiday spirit, Ben twisted away from the front door and saw Mike and Ellen coming down the stairs. "Merry Christmas, guys. Coffee's in the kitchen, and we're waiting in the family room to open gifts."

"We'll be right in," Ellen replied.

Once they were all together and had refilled their coffee from the carafe that Ellen and Julie thoughtfully set up on the bar, they took turns handing out and opening gifts.

They had all agreed that they wouldn't bring large or bulky gifts to England, since it would only mean having to take them back in their luggage, so all the gifts were small, including quite a few envelopes.

Sam loved the new Kindle Oasis that Rob and Ben gave her. She'd dropped her Kindle Paperwhite a few months earlier, cracked the corner of the screen, and hadn't replaced it yet. Mike and Ellen cooed over the gift certificate to Bourbon Steak in DC from Ben and Rob. It was Mike's favorite restaurant in the city.

The voucher for a trip to Florida from Sam's travel agency that Ben and Rob gave Julie made her squeal in delight. She could go and visit her family again whenever she liked. She ran over and hugged them both tightly.

"Thank you so much!" she exclaimed. "Mom will be so happy."

Jon praised Rob and Ben for the scarf and silver Christmas ornament, saying it was too much since they had welcomed him into their celebration. In turn, he'd given them a gift card to a favorite restaurant in Westport that Sam had suggested, since they visited it often.

When Ben reached for the box next to him, Rob paused and looked at him, smiling.

Rob thought back to the day he walked into the Artistic Alchemist to discuss a Christmas gift for Ben. Matt showed him sketches of several jewelry designs, and Rob had lit up as soon as he saw the drawing of this bracelet. Matt's design artfully combined platinum and leather with a clasp featuring a compass rose. Rob used his wedding ring to make a bracelet for himself and had a new bracelet made for Ben. This way, they'd have matching bracelets, but Rob would still be able to carry part of Alan with him. The insides of the bracelets were both inscribed with "Here's to new adventures!", along with the date Ben and Rob met—10.03.2019. The compass on Ben's bracelet had a small round diamond—his birthstone—in the center, while Rob's featured a ruby.

After removing the paper, Ben opened the cover of the plain black box and saw the beautiful bracelet nestled in a bed of red tissue paper. "Oh my God, it's gorgeous." He carefully lifted it up and read the inscription inside. A tear trickled down his cheek, and he leaned over and kissed Rob tenderly. "I love you so much."

Rob reached into the pocket of his pajama pants and pulled out a nearly identical one. "Um, I may have gotten one for myself too."

"Of course you did." Ben laughed. Wearing matching sappy grins, they took turns placing the bracelets on each other's wrists.

With hopeful anticipation, Ben found the envelope he'd brought for Rob and handed it to him. "You're so difficult to buy for, sweetie. I hope you like it."

Rob opened the envelope and pulled out the gorgeous Christmas card Ben had painstakingly searched for. Inside was a note from Ben explaining that they were leaving on

Monday to fly to Barcelona where they'd relive their meeting a year earlier. They were staying at the same hotel, and Ben had even made reservations for a spa day.

"It's perfect," Rob said, choking up. "I can't believe you did this."

He hugged Ben and kissed him hard.

"Do I have to tell you two to get a room?" Kyle teased, clearly pleased at their affection for each other.

"Thanks, but I already have one," Rob replied, waving the note and laughing. He turned to Ben, then Sam. "So I guess this is why I never saw the return flight information for this trip, huh?"

"Oh my goodness, Rob!" Sam said, a stern look on her face that quickly morphed into a teasing smile. "It's so hard to surprise you because you insist on knowing everything. Sometimes you just need to let it go."

"I'm duly chastised and will do my best to not have to know everything." Rob looked chagrined, but Ben was pretty sure he wasn't planning on changing anytime soon.

"Here's a little something extra," Sam chimed in, handing an envelope to Ben.

Ben opened it, revealing a certificate for a private tour of Sagrada Familia.

"This is too much," he protested.

"Nonsense," Sam shot back. "You deserve it. Besides, you said you never got there last year. Just go and enjoy yourselves."

"Thank you, Sam," Rob and Ben said in unison. "We will."

"Well, it looks like that's it for the gifts," Mike declared. "How about we all have some breakfast?"

THEY ENDED up eating a late breakfast, so no one was hungry at lunchtime, but around one o'clock Rob and Sam found the makings for a charcuterie board in the fridge. After a bit of slicing and dicing, they set it on the bar along with some plates and cutlery, so that folks could pick at it during the afternoon.

Mrs. Harrison arrived around four and began her last-minute tasks for dinner. As instructed, Ben had placed the prepped turkey in the oven at the recommended time and temperature earlier in the day. Mrs. H had left clear instructions as to when to start the turkey so that everything would be ready on time. To accompany the bird, there would be roasted potatoes with carrots and parsnips, Brussels sprouts, Yorkshire pudding, herb stuffing, and cranberry sauce. And of course, gravy and bread sauce.

At Ben's insistence, Mrs. Harrison set another place at the dining table for herself. She'd planned to make a plate for herself and eat in the kitchen, but they all balked at that idea. She would celebrate with them in the dining room, and that was that.

With everything in the kitchen under control, Mrs. Harrison joined their group in the family room to relax and chat over drinks before dinner.

AS THEY SAT at the dining table, Ben noticed that Mrs. H had included colorful Christmas crackers at each place setting. As was the tradition, they each pulled one open and took turns reading the joke or riddle that each cracker contained. They proudly displayed the little toy or trinket that was also inside, and they all donned their festive paper hats for dinner.

The meal was exquisite. Everything was cooked to perfection—they all toasted Mrs. H and her stellar culinary skills. Dessert was a Christmas pudding that she'd made weeks ago and brought to them. They also had small mince pies that one of the other town ladies had made the day before, and a treacle tart like those that Ben and Mike both remembered from their childhood.

Once they had all eaten themselves into a food coma, they pushed their chairs back to relax at the table while they reminisced about past Christmases over wine or a snifter of brandy.

"More wine, Mrs. H, or some brandy, perhaps?" Mike asked.

"No, thank you, Master Michael. I still need to drive home," she told them.

"One of us can take you home," Ben said.

Mrs. Harrison waved away his suggestion. "None of that now, Master Ben. This has been quite lovely, but I'll just clean up the kitchen and then be on my way."

"I've got a better idea, Mrs. H," Ben said. "Why don't you and Mike and Ellen retire to the family room and listen to some Christmas music while the rest of us clean up? You've done more than enough for us. And I'll bring out some tea for you to enjoy while you all relax."

And with that, they pitched in and had the food put away and the dishwasher filled in record time.

CHAPTER 15

Saturday, December 26 – Boxing Day

The group was just finishing up breakfast when the doorbell rang.

"I'll get it," said Ben as he turned and left the kitchen.

He opened the door to find Mrs. Harrison standing there holding a covered platter.

"Why Mrs. H, what brings you here on this fine and sunny day?" It was indeed a beautiful day. Cold but not bone chillingly, so and the sky was a brilliant, cloudless blue.

"I just wanted to say thanks again for a lovely Christmas celebration yesterday, Master Ben. I made you all some sausage rolls for Boxing Day." She presented him with the platter, continuing, "Now I'm off to Millie Feeney's. A few of us get together for tea and a chat every now and then. Enjoy your day."

"Thank you so much, Mrs. H. I'm so grateful for your thoughtfulness. We'll certainly enjoy them while watching football this afternoon."

Boxing Day landed on a Saturday that year, and even though the bank holiday was officially celebrated on Monday, there were lots of local teams and many professional ones who had football matches scheduled over the weekend. In fact, a couple of local school teams were playing in the field at the edge of the park that afternoon, and some of the group had decided to watch them play.

Ben returned to the kitchen with the platter and told everyone of Mrs. Harrison's generosity.

"That's very nice of her," Rob said. He was slicing some of the leftover turkey from Christmas dinner while Sam and Julie were assembling a cheese platter with some fruit and vegetables plus a large bowl of salad. Their plan was to get everything ready now, so that the rest of the day would be relaxed and casual for everyone.

Ben's cell phone buzzed, and he excused himself to check his messages. "Alex said that he should be here shortly after noon. Once he gets here, we can have a quick bite if he's hungry, then head into town for some football. We should be back in time for the match on the telly later this afternoon."

Rob glanced over and smiled at him. The longer he was in England, the more Ben slipped into a bit of an accent, his speech becoming peppered with British terms like "telly." It was so cute. He really had it bad for this guy.

A couple of hours later, they were all sitting around in the family room when they heard the doorbell. When Ben answered, Alex stood there with a case of beer under his arm and a broad smile on his face. It reminded Ben of their time together in secondary school when Alex would come to visit—without the case of beer, of course.

"Merry Christmas, mate," he said, handing the ale to Ben.

"And to you," Ben replied, peering over Alex's shoulder. "You didn't bring Jeremy?"

"No. It's not serious between us—at least not yet. He's spending a few days with his fam up north."

"C'mon in, everyone's in the family room." As Ben was leading Alex down the hall, the bell rang again, so he handed the beer back to Alex. "Just take this in, please, while I answer the door."

Sheila was standing on the top step with a bottle of wine. "Merry Christmas, Ben."

"Merry Christmas to you, Sheila. I'm so glad you made it."

They joined everyone else, and after introductions were made, talked about what they would do next.

Sam and Julie both decided to stay at the house, as they weren't really into football all that much and preferred to stay warm and cozy. The rest of them bundled up and grabbed a few sausage rolls to munch along the way as they left for town.

A FEW HOURS LATER, Rob arrived back at The Mews to find Sam and Julie in front of the fire in the family room. Sam was reading on her new Kindle, and Julie was working on a piece of needlepoint.

"Back already?" Julie asked. "Where are the others?"

"They'll be along shortly, I imagine. I left early 'cause it was a bit too cold for me. I was afraid my toes were going to fall off," Rob joked.

"Well, come sit near the fire and warm up," Sam offered.

"I will once I get myself a drink." Rob went to the bar and poured a generous shot of Woodford Reserve over some ice.

Sitting next to Sam on the sofa, he took a sip and sighed with pleasure. "Ah, that hits the spot. What are you reading?"

"Another book in that cozy mystery series you got me hooked on."

"Hey, blame Ben. He started me on that last year when we met."

"Actually, I think it might have been my fault," Julie interrupted. "You're talking about the Cozy Corgi series by Mildred Abbott, right?"

When both Sam and Rob nodded, she continued, "I'm the one that got Ben started on those a couple of years ago. But since it sounds like you both really like them, you're welcome." There was a twinkle in her eye.

"I don't mind at all," Rob confessed. "I read a lot, so I'm always looking for something new. Feel free to send any recommendations my way."

"Happily. What do you like to read?" Julie asked.

"I'll give pretty much anything a try, but my favorites are mystery and suspense. I'll also read paranormal, romance, and sci-fi. If there are gay characters, so much the better."

"Cool. I'll send you a list of some of my favorite authors and their books. But this goes both ways. You've got to send me your favorites too."

"I don't have as much time to read as I'd like, but I think I want in on this," Sam joined in. "I'd rather read something that one of you recommends than just pick something at random on Amazon."

"Deal," Rob said. "This is gonna be fun."

AN HOUR OR SO LATER, the rest of the group returned home. They'd converted the bar into a makeshift buffet with sliced turkey and stuffing for sandwiches, a cheese platter with some fruit and vegetables, a large salad, and Mrs. Harrison's delicious sausage rolls.

Mike found a football match on the television, and they settled in to enjoy. It was the perfect end to a perfect day.

CHAPTER 16

Sunday, December 27 – The Mews and Winchester

When Ben and Rob ambled into the kitchen, they were pleased to see that everyone else was already there enjoying coffee and chatting about their plans for the next day or two. Mike and Ellen were flying home on Tuesday morning, but the rest of the group had flights to the States on Monday.

"I wanted to tell you something," Ben began. "As wonderful as it's been to spend time with all of you for the past week or so, Rob and I have decided to leave a day early. We're driving up to Winchester after lunch today. We stopped there for lunch at the beginning of this trip and were hoping to get back sometime in the last week, but that never happened. We figured we'd do it today."

"But Winchester's only an hour or so away," Mike said. "Are you heading back to London today?"

"No," answered Rob. "Ben got us accommodations at the Wykeham Arms in Winchester for tonight. I really wanted to visit the cathedral, so we'll do that this afternoon and then stay overnight. Our flight to Barcelona isn't until one o'clock tomorrow; that gives us plenty of time to get to Heathrow in the morning."

"Mike, can you call Sheila and remind her of when you all are leaving?" Ben asked. "She'll get a team in to empty the fridge, wash the linens, and clean the whole house. I'm pretty sure they'll also take down all the decorations and store the boxes back in the carriage house. You should also ask her if she can recommend an estate agent to handle the sale of your portion of the house to Rob. We'll probably also need a solicitor to take care of a few things. She might have a suggestion on who would be able to do that."

Ben had spoken earlier in the week with Kyle and Julie about what had transpired between him and Mike, so everyone was aware of the fact that Rob and Ben would soon own The Mews together.

"Of course," Mike agreed. "And there's no rush to do everything. I'll get the ball rolling, and then we can take care of the details once we're all back in the States. The firm I work for has had dealings with a few law offices here in England, so they may be able to facilitate some of the process."

"Great. Let us know what needs to be done, and we'll make it happen," Ben told him. "Even if it means another trip over here."

"I'm not sure that will be necessary, but I'll let you know."

WHEN THEY WERE DONE with lunch, Rob and Ben retrieved the now-packed luggage from their bedroom and brought it out to the car. Back inside, there were lots of hugs and kisses and a few tears, but they'd see everyone again when they were all back home, so there was no reason to be sad.

As Ben pulled out of the driveway, Rob opened the Maps app on Ben's phone and typed in the address for the Wykeham Arms. The weather was clear, the sky was cerulean, the drive was pleasant and uneventful.

After finding a car park around the corner from the pub where they'd be staying, they towed their roller bags over the cobblestone walk and checked in to their room. They quickly freshened up and headed out to explore the town.

They spent a fair amount of time at the famous Winchester Cathedral, both in the main building itself and meandering around the grounds.

"This place is magnificent," Rob said in awe. "I did a bit of research yesterday once I knew we were really coming here. There's a guided tour as well as a self-guided one."

Ben smiled at Rob's enthusiasm. He loved how excited he got when visiting new places. "We can do whatever you want, love."

"I know we don't have a lot of time, but I also know that we can come back again the next time we stay at the house. I think for today, I want to visit the crypt and see the Sound II sculpture. I'd also like to visit Jane Austen's tomb."

So that's what they did.

Later, they wandered around town a bit, walking through

the Abbey Gardens, along part of High Street and The Square. It was chilly, but the exercise felt good—they were used to being a bit more active and had gotten lax while staying at The Mews.

Eventually, they made their way back to Kingsgate and the Wykeham Arms. Finding a table in the pub, they relaxed over a couple of pints of Fuller's Ale.

"This has been a really fantastic day," Rob said, his voice bubbling with excitement. "I remember listening to the song 'Winchester Cathedral' when I was growing up, but I never expected that I'd actually see it one day. Thanks for bringing me here."

"Of course, sweetheart. I must admit, aside from having lunch here with you last week, I hadn't been here in years, so I've enjoyed it too. Plus, I love how excited you get when you visit new places. Your enthusiasm spills over, and I feel it."

Rob reached out to touch the bracelet on Ben's wrist. "Do you really like it?" Rob asked, sounding a bit unsure.

"I love it. It really sums us up and will always remind me of how we met. Did Matthew design these?"

"He did. I went to his shop to find something to get you for Christmas. But I also wanted to talk to him about my wedding ring—"

"I know you haven't worn it for a while," Ben interrupted. "I thought about saying something to you about it but wasn't really sure how to phrase it without sounding weird. I don't mind if you wear it, you know. I know you still love Alan, but I also know that you love me too. It's okay."

Rob stared into Ben's eyes, a look of complete adoration clearly on his face.

"Thank you, sweetheart. Matthew actually came up with solutions for both your gift *and* my ring." Rob stroked his own bracelet. He slid his finger over the compass rose clasp. "This is my wedding ring. Matthew melted the platinum and added a bit more metal before reworking it into this. Then he made yours to match."

"Oh my God, that's fantastic!" Ben declared. "That's a perfect solution."

"It is," Rob said. Ben loved how content Rob looked in that moment. "Matthew showed me several sketches of his designs, and as soon as I saw this bracelet, I knew it was perfect for us."

They chatted a bit more before Rob said, "Okay, all that earlier exercise has made me hungry. Do you want to split the Cobble Lane charcuterie board to start? Then I'm thinking of getting the loin of pork for dinner."

"That sounds great. I think I'll have the sirloin of beef for my entrée. And two more pints? Or would you prefer some wine?" Ben asked.

"Hmmm, another pint, please."

<hr>

LATER THAT NIGHT while they were both lying in bed, Rob turned to Ben. "This has been such a great trip. We've done so much already, and it's not even over yet. I can't believe that we're going back to Barcelona, and we're gonna relive some of what we did a year ago. You're the best boyfriend ever. I love you."

"I love you too," Ben confessed, breathless. "And I think

you're the best boyfriend. Thank you for being there for me after my blow up with Mike and for coming up with a solution. You don't know how much that means to me, love."

"We're here for each other, darling. Always."

Monday, December 28 – Barcelona

As they landed at Barcelona's El Prat Airport, Rob couldn't help but think of a year earlier. He'd been exhausted and a bit out of sorts starting a vacation that he really wasn't ready for. How different he felt now, sitting next to the man he loved.

Smiling, he reached over and took Ben's hand. "I can't believe we're back here. Thank you."

"Of course, darling. As I told you on Christmas morning, you're extremely difficult to buy for. It's even harder to surprise you with anything. But after discussing it with Sam, I knew this would be perfect for both of us."

Once they retrieved their luggage and went through customs, they exited and were met by several drivers, all holding placards displaying names. They quickly spotted their driver, an attractive woman with long dark hair and a radiant smile.

"*Buenos dias, señores Rockingham y Asher,*" she said. "I am Sofia. Please follow me."

She grabbed their large roller cases, and they followed her to a black Mercedes SUV.

While she loaded the luggage into the back of the vehicle, Rob and Ben climbed into the back seat.

Once behind the wheel, Sofia said, "Just to confirm, you are going to the Hotel L17 Metropolitan on Rambla de Catalunya. Is that right?"

"*Si, por favor,*" Ben replied.

"Traffic isn't too bad right now; we should arrive there in an hour or less."

They sat back and enjoyed their ride into the city.

WHILE BEN CHECKED in at the registration desk, Rob wandered around the lobby, awash with memories from a year ago. *What a difference a year makes*, he thought. From what he could see, nothing much had changed at the hotel, but in many ways, he felt like a different man. A year ago, part of him was broken; he was scared to be traveling by himself. He felt so alone. Now he felt whole again with Ben at his side.

Ben approached him. "They're running a little behind today and need a few more minutes to get the room ready. Why don't we leave our luggage here, and they'll take it up to the room once it's all set. We can go sit in the bar and have something to drink while we wait. I'll get a text when we can pick up the key cards."

They proceeded down the hallway and were happy to see a familiar face behind the bar.

"*Señor* Ben, *señor* Rob! Welcome back!" Carlos greeted them warmly.

"*Buenas tardes,* Carlos. It's so good to see you again," Rob replied as he and Ben sat at the corner of the bar.

They shook hands with Carlos as he inquired, "What can I get for you to drink?"

"I think we need some of that wonderful tempranillo to celebrate our return," Ben answered.

As Carlos poured, he said, "I'm so pleased to see you. What brings you back, my friends?"

"We were in England for the holidays, and Ben surprised me with a mini-vacation to Barcelona as a Christmas gift. We'll be here for a few days before flying back to the States."

"I'm so happy that your friendship continued after you left us last year." He looked closely at the two of them and smiled broadly. "But it's more than just friendship, isn't it?"

"That it is, Carlos," Ben said, taking Rob's hand where it rested on the bar. "It seemed only right to celebrate our anniversary here."

"Most excellent, *señores*. In that case, the wine is on me. *¡Feliz aniversario!*"

"Thank you, Carlos," they said together, lifted their glasses in a toast, and drank.

"It's as good as I remember it," Rob said, grinning. "Perhaps even a bit better."

THE ALARM on Ben's phone buzzed, and he quickly silenced it. They were in the same room that Rob had occupied a year earlier. Ben had specifically requested it.

Rolling over, he looked at Rob and beamed. "That nap felt good, didn't it?"

"It definitely did. Even short flights seem to wipe me out these days. And after that glass of wine, a little nap was exactly what I needed."

Rob leaned forward and kissed Ben lightly. Which turned into another kiss. And then another, this time not so gentle. Ben ran his tongue along the seam of Rob's lips, and Rob willingly opened to him. Their tongues dueled, taking turns giving and receiving until they were both breathless.

Rob clutched Ben's ass and pulled him closer, feeling his hardness against his own thickening cock.

"Do we have time?" he asked, panting.

"Why don't we shower together? That way we can get dirty and clean at the same time."

"You always have the best ideas." Rob grinned.

They stripped quickly, and Ben sank to his knees under the shower's spray. Rob was fully erect, and Ben swallowed him to the root. Easing off a little, he circled the head of Rob's cock with his tongue and then licked at the slit, collecting the precum that was pooling there.

Rob moaned as Ben sucked eagerly, moving his hand behind Rob's balls and teasing his hole.

"Not gonna last," Rob cried as the tip of Ben's finger breached him.

Using his other hand to stroke Rob's dick, Ben flicked his tongue at the head, knowing how much it excited Rob.

"Oh God. Coming!" Rob shouted while Ben enveloped the head of Rob's cock with his mouth and swallowed greedily.

Rob panted as his spent cock slipped from Ben's lips. After a few moments of recovery, he pushed at Ben's shoulder, so that he'd fall back. Ben landed on his ass, his still-hard dick pointing straight up.

Rob grabbed a small bottle of lube from the soap rack and dripped some onto Ben's cock.

"How did that get in here?" Ben asked with a snort.

"I might have put it here. You know, just in case." Rob winked as he snaked his hand behind his back to prep himself.

Kneeling across Ben's lap, he lowered himself onto Ben's rigid staff until he was fully seated.

"You feel so good inside me." Rob panted, slowly riding Ben, gradually picking up speed. He leaned down and kissed Ben deeply, and Ben began to suck on his tongue.

Rob angled his hips slightly and continued to impale himself on Ben's cock.

"That's it," he exclaimed, breaking the kiss. "Right there!"

Ben's breath quickened. "*Ughnhm.*"

He came hard, spilling into Rob's ass. Rob slowed his pace, falling to the side and resting against the side of the large shower stall.

"Wow!"

"Couldn't have said it better myself."

After resting a few moments, they slowly got to their feet and began to lather each other, washing away the sweat and cum.

AFTERWARD, they wandered down *Rambla de Catalunya*, heading away from *La Plaça de Catalunya*.

"So tapas for dinner, huh?" Rob asked, a twinkle in his eye.

"Well, it was kinda our first date, so I thought it was appropriate. We'll go to the spa tomorrow and have dinner at that great seafood restaurant. What better way to celebrate than to recreate those first days we spent together, right?"

"I love it. And I love you. As great as Christmas was in England with everyone, I'm having the best time just doing all of this again with you."

With that, they turned into the entrance for Taller de Tapas, and Ben approached the hostess to see if there were seats available at the bar.

***

Tuesday, December 29, Barcelona

THEY SPENT A FANTASTIC DAY TOGETHER, including a luxurious and relaxing few hours at the spa, reminiscent of the special time they'd shared a year ago. Dinner was amazing: grilled shrimp and *jamón* with tomato bread, branzino, and wine. Lots of wine.

As they entered their hotel room, Rob turned on the light. "This was the best day ever, Ben. I know I say it a lot, but I love you so much."

"I love you too. But there's one thing left to do to make this day complete."

Ben lowered himself to one knee and looked up at Rob as

he pulled a small black velvet box from his pocket. Rob gasped, tucking his hand over his mouth when realization hit him.

"You've made me happier than I ever expected I could be," Ben said, sincerity dotting his words. "I never thought I'd meet someone like you. Sweetheart, I don't ever want to be without you in my life. Will you do me the honor of becoming my husband?"

Rob's eyes grew to the size of saucers. He smiled widely as tears fell from his eyes. "Of course, I will. You're everything to me."

Pulling Ben up off the floor, he hugged and kissed him, pouring all the love he felt for this man into the kiss. It was time to start the next phase of his life … his life with Ben.

The End

F*riday, December 25 – Christmas night, Jon's room*

Jon exited the bathroom he shared with Kyle and crawled under the covers. After a moment, he heard Kyle in the bathroom. It sounded like he was brushing his teeth.

After a couple of minutes, his side of the bathroom door opened, and Kyle stepped into the room, wearing only a pair of dark boxer briefs.

"Merry Christmas, Jon," he said, joining him in bed. Jon reached for him, pulling him tightly to his hirsute chest, and kissed him deeply.

They rolled together, stopping with Jon on top, and he ground his thickening dick against Kyle's already hard member.

"God, you feel so good," he panted between kisses.

"You do too," Kyle replied, grabbing Jon's ass. "Can't believe I'm finally here with you."

"Well, it hasn't really been easy to spend much time together since someone's always around. Although I must admit, I didn't expect anything like this to happen when I agreed to come here with Sam."

"I wasn't expecting this either, but I'm certainly not complaining." Kyle beamed at him.

Jon hugged Kyle tightly and pressed their lips together again, probing his mouth and swiping at Kyle's tongue.

"God, I love how you taste," Jon sighed, peppering kisses down Kyle's chest.

He tongued Kyle's navel, and the coarse hair from his treasure trail tickled Jon's lips. He breathed against Kyle's rigid length, then slowly pulled down the front of his boxer briefs and tucked the waistband behind Kyle's hairy balls. Inhaling Kyle's musky scent, Jon licked his cock from root to tip.

Kyle sighed, and Jon continued his ministrations, sucking on the silky head and hollowing his cheeks as he took him deeper. Kyle pulled him back up and kissed him again, sliding his tongue along the seam of Jon's lips until Jon opened to him. Their tongues twisted together, and they moaned into each other's mouths.

After several minutes of hot and heavy kissing, Kyle said, "I want to taste you."

Moving Jon around and onto his back, Kyle spun and straddled him so that his own cock hovered over Jon's mouth as he faced Jon's uncut dick.

Jon greedily took Kyle to the back of his throat while Kyle slipped his tongue between the head of Jon's cock and his foreskin.

"Mmmm," he hummed, twirling his tongue around the crown and gathering up the precum there.

Jon gently sucked on Kyle's balls before moving back to his furry crease. He teased Kyle's pucker, then plunged his tongue into Kyle's hole.

"Ungh," Kyle panted. Pulling Jon's foreskin back, he licked around the sensitive head, then swallowed him down to the root. He continued moving up and down the shaft, gradually picking up speed.

Jon moved back to Kyle's cock, using his fingers to tease his rim as he nipped and bathed the head of Kyle's dick.

"I'm close," Kyle whispered, briefly pulling off Jon's cock, then going back to sucking as he pulled on Jon's balls.

Kyle's sac tightened, and he came, spilling his load down Jon's throat.

Jon hummed around the dick filling his mouth, doing his best to drink down every drop. Kyle redoubled his efforts, moving faster and faster until he was rewarded with Jon's release.

As their breathing slowed, Kyle moved around and up so that he and Jon were once again face-to-face. They kissed, tasting themselves on each other's lips.

"That was amazing," Jon said.

"Yeah, it was," Kyle agreed. "Is it okay if I stay?"

"Please," replied Jon. "I love to cuddle."

"I do too." Kyle turned over, becoming the little spoon. Jon hugged him tight against his chest, and they drifted off to sleep.

Join Kyle and Jon as they fall in love in *Love On The Potomac*, available now. It features an age gap romance, low angst, and a romantic river cruise.

You can get it here:

https://books2read.com/potomac

A LETTER FROM RJ

Dear Reader,

Thank you so much for reading Love for the Holidays. The next book in this series is Love on the Potomac. Find out what happens when Kyle and Jon decide to try a long distance relationship. But eventually Kyle will need to tell his Dad—who may have issues with the fact that Jon is thirteen years older than Kyle.

Be sure to follow me on Amazon to be notified of new releases, and look for me on Facebook for sneak peeks of upcoming stories.

Please take a moment to write a review of Love for the Holidays on Amazon and Goodreads. Reviews can make all the difference in helping a book show up in Amazon searches.

To to sign up for my newsletter, stop by rj-peterson.ck.page.

We have a great reader group on Facebook that can be found here: www.facebook.com/groups/rjpetersonsadventurers/

Finally, several of my titles are available on audio, narrated by the amazing Kevin Earlywine or the fabulous Cole Kurtz. They can be found here: link.rjpeterson.net/audio

Happy reading!

RJ

P.S. Keep going for a free download!

FREE SHORT STORY

Download a copy of His Elevator Pitch

Inspired by a writing prompt, His Elevator Pitch is the story of River, an unemployed executive assistant, and Thom, the department head of a prestigious multi-faceted corporation.

When a power failure takes out several city blocks in Boston, MA, they find themselves stuck in an elevator with nothing but time on their hands.

Conversation ensues and when power is restored, River goes off to his interview, thinking that's the end of his encounter with the handsome stranger. Or is it?

This story features many of the themes my writing is known for: older guys, sweet-with-heat encounters, low or no angst, and always a happily ever after.

SCAN THE CODE TO DOWNLOAD

About the Author

Hi, I'm RJ! I'm a retired graphic designer. An avid reader—preferably while sipping a vodka martini or bourbon on the rocks—I've had a long and varied career, including library page, car wash attendant, travel agent, and graphic designer in the marijuana industry. In addition, I worked in the banking industry for twenty-five years. I love to travel and have been on 60+ cruises. When not on a cruise, my husband & I live in New England.

I never planned to be a writer, but a fateful day in January, 2021 changed it all. I woke with a story stuck in my head and started typing. The more I type, the more story ideas I get.

Find all my links here:

WANT TO READ MORE?

The New Adventures in Love Series:

Love On The Horizon

Love For The Holidays

Love On The Potomac

Love In The Mediterranean

Love Is For Family

(Coming in 2025)

Hawthorne Bluff Series:

Finding Finlay

Addicted to Ashton

Chasing Courtland

(Coming in 2026)

SEAsons of Love Series:

Love at Frost Sight

Resting Grinch Face

Don't Claus a Scene

Great Chemis-Tree

Stand Alone Stories

The Locket's Tale

Footprints on My Heart

(Coming in 2025)

All my book links in one place!